Weddings by Saffronella

PATRINA McKENNA

Also by Patrina McKenna

Romantic comedy with a twist!

Truelove Hills
Truelove Hills – Mystery at Pebble Cove
Truelove Hills – The Matchmaker
Granny Prue's Bucket List
Christmas with the Neighbours
Trouble at Featherlow Forbes Menswear
Lady Featherlow's Tea Room
Christmas in Featherlow Bottom
Weddings by Saffronella

Feel good fantasy for all the family!

GIANT Gemstones
A Galaxy of Gemstones
The Gemstone Dynasty
Enrico's Journey
Summer Camp at Tadgers Blaney Manor

DEDICATION

For my family and friends

1

A NEW CAREER

Saffronella Hamilton-Smythe unlocked the door to the summer house in her parents' garden. Today was the first day of her new career. So far, she had drifted between one tedious job to another, but this time she was sure she'd found the right one. At twenty-five and an expert on weddings – she'd been to eight over the last two years – Saffie had come up with the brightest of ideas; she had everything it took to be a Wedding Planner.

It was a bit embarrassing still living at home with her parents, but with hard work and determination, Saffie was sure she'd have enough money to buy an apartment in London before long. In the meantime, it was convenient living in leafy Kensington; her parents were overseas for most of the time, and, as an only child, she had the family home to herself. Using the summer house overlooking the lake for her new business premises had been another bright idea.

Saffie sat down in the white leather swivel chair and spun around. Never before had she been so excited about going to work. This job would be a doddle; she already had a list of nine potential clients to call. The Hamilton-Smythes had a vast network of contacts, and her mother had advised a few of her friends about Saffie's new business. She leant forward on the desk and dialled the number at the top of the list.

'Good morning, it's Saffronella here. I'm London's newest Wedding Planner ... Yes, that's right, I'm Vivienne's daughter ... What? A portfolio of my experience? ... How will I get experience if you don't give me a chance? ... My mother wouldn't recommend me if she didn't know I could do it ... Well, that's very disappointing ... I'm sorry to have wasted your time. Goodbye.'

Saffie took a deep breath. That wasn't a good start; she'd need to try a different tactic with the next client.

'Hello, I'm Saffronella – your Wedding Planner of choice. Just let me know the date of your wedding, and I'll do everything for you. I'm very experienced ... Two years' time ... The Maldives ... You want *me* to manage the budget? ... Twelve bridesmaids ... Hen Do in Ibiza

…' Saffronella rubbed her forehead, trust the Bloomfields to go over the top for their daughter's wedding. 'I need to stop you there, Mrs Bloomfield. Those dates clash with another event I'm organising. I'm very sorry, but I can't offer you my services on this occasion. It was nice talking to you. Goodbye.'

Saffie flopped back in her chair. Maybe she hadn't thought this concept through. She was about to give up on her bright idea – until she had another one. Two of Saffie's friends were walking around the lake carrying a tray of drinks. Sophie and Clare had stayed over last night. Saffie drummed her fingers on her desk. Her friends were intelligent women, far too good to be working in boring office jobs. She sat up as they entered the summer house.

Sophie smiled. 'We thought you'd be ready for an iced coffee by now. How's your first morning going?'

Clare perched herself on a windowsill. 'You need to get some chairs in here for your clients.'

Saffie stood up. 'Here, try my chair for size.'

Clare walked around the white marble desk and sank into the luxurious leather chair. She swivelled around enjoying the view. The octagonal summer house had windows on all sides. There was the lake, the house, the tennis court, the outdoor pool with an electric canopy for when it rained. Saffie had undoubtedly been born with a silver spoon in her mouth. Clare allowed herself a wry smile; her friend had used that spoon to dig herself out of many catastrophes over the years. Hopefully, her latest venture would prove fruitful.

Sophie sat on the end of the desk. 'So, go on tell us, how many clients have signed up for your services?'

'None yet. That's where my two best friends in the world come in.'

Clare and Sophie looked at one another. Clare raised an eyebrow. 'Who might *they* be?'

'You two, of course. The three of us have been together since we were eleven. What's that? Fifteen years?'

Sophie raised her eyes to the ceiling. 'That would make us twenty-six, and we're all twenty-five. Your maths has always been shocking.'

'Exactly! I would never have passed all those Finance exams like Clare did. Or even started the Business Management course you scraped through, Sophie. But I didn't need to. You both have the brains, and I have the . . .'

Clare stood up. 'Don't you even dare say "beauty" – you may have long blonde hair and a figure to die for, but, at the end of the day, you don't have a job.'

Saffie lowered her pale violet eyes. 'That's very harsh. Will you two help me, or not?'

Clare sat back down in the white swivel chair. 'What's in it for us?'

'I'll pay you by the hour for the time you spend helping me on each wedding. I'll do all the front work: Speak to the clients, visit the venues, meet with suppliers, go to the weddings. I just need help with the office work: Managing the budgets, paying the suppliers, ordering the stationery, checking all the details on the invitations, table plans etc.' Saffie held her arms in the air. 'Basically, I need support and encouragement to get my new career off the ground – preferably from you two.'

Clare shot a glance at Sophie. "New career?" Saffronella didn't have a career to speak of in the first place. They were both surprised to hear her talk like this; it sounded like she had put some thought into the role of Wedding Planner – she also knew her limitations.

Sophie winked at Clare before speaking to Saffie, 'Why don't you go and get us more drinks while Clare and I think about your proposal?'

Saffie smiled as she opened the door. 'I'll bring snacks as well. Thanks, girls! I couldn't do this without you.'

As soon as Saffie was out of earshot, Clare leant on the desk. 'She sounds serious about this. Why don't we help her with her first wedding? It won't be too much work if the three of us join forces. She needs to start her new business from somewhere.'

Sophie picked up the list of names and telephone numbers. The first two potential clients had been crossed through. She handed it to Clare. 'Jamie Coolridge and Laura Fulgrove are on here. They're getting married in July.'

Clare's mouth fell open. 'Wow, that's next month! I'm surprised they haven't hired a Wedding Planner by now.'

Sophie sighed. 'I heard they've been bickering for months. They can't agree on anything to do with their wedding.'

Clare's eyes widened. 'Saffie could sort those two out. She can be very persuasive.'

Saffie pushed the door open with her back as she held onto a tray of diet cokes and fresh cream chocolate éclairs. 'Here we go, ladies. Nourishment to get us through our first morning working together.'

Clare picked up an éclair and nodded towards Sophie, who spoke on their behalf, 'We'll help you with your first wedding. We'll fit the hours in around our day jobs.'

Saffie squealed with delight. 'I knew you would! We now need to find a couple that'll let us loose on planning their big day.'

Sophie handed the list to Saffie. 'We've found just the one. We've highlighted them on here.'

Saffie snorted. 'Jamie Coolridge! I used to go out with him.'

Clare put the éclair down and wiped her hands on a tissue. 'We know. It's the perfect challenge for you to get your teeth into. They're desperate, and the wedding's next month. Trust you to start your new job on a Saturday when we're both available to help. Make the call now, and by the end of the weekend, Wedding Number One will be well and truly underway.'

2

AN OLD ACQUAINTANCE

Clare and Sophie carried two gold brocade dining room chairs around the lake. Clare's shoulders ached under the weight. 'I'm going to the gym tonight to cancel my membership. Saffie's already got us doing manual work, and we're only an hour into our new jobs.'

Sophie chuckled. 'She didn't get us to do anything. It was our idea to bring chairs into her office. It wouldn't look good if her first bride and groom had to sit on the floor.'

Clare placed her chair on the grass and stretched her arms as she nodded towards the summer house. 'If it were anyone other than Saffie attempting to do this, I'd be off before her nails dried.'

Sophie placed her chair on the grass too. 'You have to be kidding me! She's sitting at her desk painting her nails. I thought she'd at least be doing some research. Isn't she nervous?'

Clare picked up the unwieldy chair. 'Have you ever known our good friend to be nervous?'

Sophie shook her head. 'I'm just pleased it's Jamie Coolridge she's going to practise her wedding skills on. He'd eat out of her hand, given half a chance. You don't think seeing her again will put a stop to the nuptials, do you?'

Clare glanced over her shoulder as she strode ahead. 'Definitely not. Saffie's not going to look a gift horse in the mouth. Jamie's family's loaded. She'll wrap him around her little finger, get him to agree to all of Laura Fulgrove's wishes, and charge them at a premium for her last-minute services. She'll advise that all their stresses and strains will be washed away as soon as they hand over a hefty deposit.'

Sophie's eyes popped. 'That's a brilliant way of handling things. You should point Saffie in that direction.'

Clare turned and winked. 'I already have.'

*

9

Laura Fulgrove handed Saffie a heavy white folder before glaring at her fiancé. 'I've been planning my wedding since I was a little girl. I bought my wedding dress before I even met Jamie, and my six best friends have been watching their weight for the last three years. I couldn't resist buying the most exquisite bridesmaid dresses in peacock blue. I chose the same size for everyone. Only one of them has had a problem with that as she's had to bulk up. The rest have been moaning more than is necessary.'

Jamie glanced sideways at his bride. 'I think you're being very unfair. The poor girls have been on diets since we met. I'm not sure some of them will be speaking to you by next month. They won't have the energy; they're malnourished.'

Saffie leant forward on her desk. 'I can see Laura's point. When you find the perfect dress, it's hard not to make a purchase. Peacock blue is such a stunning colour. Not far from the shade of your eyes, Jamie.' Jamie blushed, and Saffie continued, 'I can take away the stress of the bridesmaid dresses from this moment on. Just send your bridesmaids, and their dresses, over to me. I'll work a little magic that means your very best friends can eat a burger or two to get their spirits up in time for your wedding. They need to be on top form for your special day.'

Laura's eyes widened. 'How will you do that?'

'I know an excellent seamstress, and with a photographer that's great at airbrushing, all your bridesmaids will look the same size in the photographs. You do have a photographer booked, don't you?'

Laura nodded. 'Of course. Jamie's parents have paid for the best. In fact, everything's booked. I really don't know why we need your services.'

Jamie lowered his head. 'My parents know Saffronella's. They thought you and I needed to loosen up a little and not be so uptight as the wedding draws closer. I must admit, I would be grateful for someone to take over the organisation of things.'

Laura grabbed hold of Jamie's knee. 'You are so thoughtful, my darling. That will give us time to focus on our honeymoon. We can pop into that delightful little boutique on Kensington High Street on our way home this afternoon. I've seen a perfect pair of white board shorts for you with little red hearts on.'

Saffie suppressed a snigger before standing up and walking around her desk. She held out her hand to shake Laura's. 'You must go and get those shorts. They sound perfect for Jamie. Just leave everything with me. I'll read through your folder and be in touch if there's anything I need clarification on.'

Saffie then turned to Jamie; she held his hand and squeezed it. 'I'll prepare some calculations and get back to you later today with my fee. Of course, I'll require a deposit. It'll need to be paid into my account by the morning.'

Jamie locked eyes with his old flame. 'Anything you say, Saffronella. It's great to be working with you.'

*

Sophie bit her fingernails as Clare pondered over the white folder. 'Is there anything we need to do, Clare? It sounds like the bride has everything in hand.'

Clare extracted a sheet from the folder and placed it in the photocopier on a table overlooking the swimming pool. 'I love this office. I could work here permanently. Views from all windows; unlimited refreshments; no work to do.' Clare handed Sophie the sheet she'd printed. 'Take a look at that and memorise it.'

Sophie read the document. 'It's a breakdown of all the wedding arrangements: Timings; contact details; costs. What?! It's costing them that much? I knew the Lavender Tree Banqueting Rooms were expensive, but not *that* expensive!'

Clare spun around in the swivel chair. 'I never thought Saffie would find her niche, but she's certainly onto a winner this time. What's a little extra money for these guys? As far as I can see, once the bridesmaids are eating again, this wedding is set to go. Saffie's business will be up and running with just the cost of a seamstress, which will be paid for by Jamie. All Saffie has to do is turn up on the day and promote her business to others. Easy peasy!'

The door to the summer house opened to the sight of Saffronella holding a bottle of champagne and three glasses. 'I've just spoken to Jamie. He was anxious to transfer a deposit to me. I had to hazard a guess, so I said £10,000. Have I been too lenient? If so, we can recoup a bit extra in our final bill. I don't think that's too bad for a day's work. Thank you for your help, girls. We should celebrate.'

With the cork popped, Saffie filled the glasses. Clare held hers in the air as she proposed a toast: 'Here's to *Weddings by Saffronella*!'

Sophie beamed as she clinked glasses with the others. 'That's a great name for Saffie's business. I'll design some business cards and stationery in the morning. With our first wedding underway, there's no time to waste!'

Saffie grinned. She liked the terminology "*our* first wedding"; it took the pressure off her. There was no need to stress when she had such capable friends as Sophie and Clare.

3

LAST-MINUTE CHANGES

Sophie flashed her ID card at the Concierge of the Lavender Tree Banqueting Rooms. 'I'm Sophie of *Weddings by Saffronella*; my colleagues will be along shortly. I need to adjust the seating plans for both the ceremony and the wedding breakfast; we've had a last-minute cancellation this morning.'

The Concierge removed his top hat. 'I'm pleased to meet you, Sophie. Follow the corridor down to your right, then take a lift to the 52nd floor. Signage is in place for the wedding of Mr Coolridge and Miss Fulgrove from there. I'm surprised we haven't seen you before.'

Sophie smiled. 'Oh, we've been dealing remotely with Miss Fulgrove on the arrangements. We're fully informed in respect of everything; we know this place like the back of our hands.' Sophie scanned the signage boards in the marble-tiled reception area. 'Could you possibly point me in the direction of the ladies' cloakroom?'

*

Sophie's heart was pounding as she applied another coat of fuchsia pink lipstick. Not only had there been a cancellation this morning, but the florist was also running late. Two guests had forgotten to mention they were vegetarian, and one of the children needed a booster seat at the dining table.

If Sophie remembered rightly, Saffie said *she'd* attend the weddings and that Sophie and Clare would do the office work. Funny how their friend had already changed her mind. To make matters worse, they had all been shopping yesterday for a team uniform. Saffie had chosen dove grey trouser suits, with white silk blouses, for Clare and Sophie and a short white skater dress for herself. When questioned about wearing white to a wedding, Saffie had shrugged and said that white was her colour, she was a Wedding Planner and she needed to blend in. Sophie's heart sank at the very thought of the look on Clare's face as they watched Saffie twirl around in the boutique.

The door to the cloakroom opened, and Clare strolled in. She looked great in her uniform. Her shoulder-length black hair had been tied back and was held in place with a stunning silver claw clip. She reached into her bag and pulled out a similar clip for Sophie. 'I knew you'd like it. I thought I'd get them as part of our uniform; Saffie can pay the bill. Turn around, and I'll do your hair the same as mine.' Sophie held up her light brown hair, and Clare clipped it in place. 'There, it's longer than mine, but not as thick. It'll hold in place OK; these clips are quite strong.'

Clare's phone buzzed, and she took it out of her bag. As she read the message, the colour drained from her face. Sophie raised her eyebrows. 'What is it?'

'It's Saffie. She's in a coffee shop with Jamie. He wants to call the wedding off.'

Sophie clenched her fists. 'It's that skater dress. We told her not to get it.'

Clare was glued to her phone. 'It's not that. Stop stressing. Saffie's still typing.'

Sophie dug her nails into the palms of her hands. 'What's she saying?'

'It sounds like last-minute nerves. Jamie says he wasn't good enough for Saffie, so how can he possibly be good enough for Laura? Wait . . . she's still typing.'

The pair waited with bated breath until the next message popped up. Clare let out a sigh of relief. 'It's back on! My guess is Jamie was chancing his arm to see if Saffie was still available, but she told him she's getting engaged next week.'

'Engaged?! She doesn't have a boyfriend.'

'I know, but good on her to turn things around with a little white lie. It would be disastrous for her business if this wedding didn't go ahead. People can be so over the top with superstition. No one would hire her.'

Sophie's phone rang, and she took the call before biting her lip and frowning at Clare. 'We need to go up to the Banqueting Rooms straight away. The bride's mother has decided to get here early to check on things.'

'Well, that's OK, isn't it? A bit of extra help won't hurt.'

'Except that she caught her heel in a groove on the stage.'

'What was she doing on the stage?'

'No idea. She's saying that one of us needs to take a taxi ride to Manolo Blahniks to buy her another pair of shoes.'

'Is that in our job description?'

Sophie linked arms with her friend. 'Come on. We

need to take a little trip first in a lift.'

'I'm not good in lifts. I'll take the stairs.'

Sophie grabbed Clare's arm. 'The lifts here are super-fast. We'll be on the roof before you know it.'

'The roof?'

'Well, the level below the roof terrace, which is also available to the wedding party.'

'This is a tall building.'

'52 floors, to be precise. Just shut your eyes and count to ten. We'll be there in no time.' Sophie had an idea. 'Once we're upstairs, there are a few adjustments to make to the seating plans and a couple of other bits that need sorting. I'll give you a thorough list to deal with before I go. I'll message you from the taxi if anything else crops up.'

Clare frowned. 'Where are you going?'

'Manolo Blahniks. I'll suffer a couple of extra journeys in the lift.' Sophie smiled to herself. There was a nice little coffee shop she could pop into on the way. She'd take a lesson from Clare's book; there was no need to stress.

4

A SUMMER WEDDING

The sun shone through the floor-to-ceiling windows of the Lavender Tree Banqueting Rooms as six bridesmaids commenced their walk down the aisle. Saffie's eyes skimmed along the narrow lavender carpet with gold embossed edges. She tutted to see the girls wearing silver shoes with their peacock blue dresses. That was a total clash with the venue's colour scheme – surely Laura should have picked up on that? If Saffie had been organising the wedding from the start, she would have noticed the mismatch of colours.

Laura made a grand entrance with her father to the sound of *Simply the Best*. Saffie smirked – that had been a last-minute change. The original song had been a classical piece. Laura glared at Saffie as she strutted past, and Saffie gave her best smile. She knew the bride was giving her a warning, but she did not need to worry. Jamie was much more suited to Laura – especially if he'd agreed to wear those board shorts on honeymoon. A plain version would have been acceptable, but white with little red hearts??

Saffie edged her way out of the room while the ceremony took place. She had some urgent things to attend to. Clare and Sophie could deal with any minor issues.

Twenty minutes later, there was a round of applause as Jamie kissed his bride. Saffie had achieved a lot in that time; manicure, facial and hair appointments were now booked for Tuesday – it was good for a girl to look her best.

After signing the register, the bride and groom walked out of the ceremony room, followed by their guests. There was a whole range of drinks and nibbles on a large circular table in the adjoining room, and Saffie held back from helping herself to a glass of champagne – she could maybe have a sneaky one later. She smirked at the sight of the bridesmaids devouring the canapés. However, she was dismayed when the very handsome videographer nudged her at the risk of ruining his shot.

Saffie kept quiet. The videographer was also recording sound. Why, oh why, were men attracted to her? Wouldn't it be nice to get to know someone without looks coming into it? Saffie had to admit that girls would die for her long blonde hair, pale violet eyes, and fantastic figure but, to her, having such assets was a curse rather than an advantage. She wished she was just boringly plain.

The videographer knocked into her again. He turned around with fire in his eyes. 'What do you think you're doing? You're ruining my shots! Give me some space, will you?'

Saffie looked down at her wet arm and legs. The woman next to her wasn't amused. 'You bumped into me! What on earth were you thinking of wearing nothing other than a white tablecloth to my niece's wedding? Serves you right it's now covered in red wine.'

Saffie was horrified, what was she going to do? This was her first wedding and now she looked a mess! How was she going to get through the rest of the day? She made a quick retreat to the ladies' cloakroom but was pulled away by a waitress before she could enter. 'You can borrow my dress. It's in my locker. Just return it at the end of the evening. Wait there a minute, and I'll fetch it for you.'

The dress was silver, strapless, tight-fitting, and six inches above the knee. Saffie counted her blessings as she zipped it up. She then opened her handbag and pulled out a stash of business cards. She planned to avoid the annoying videographer and spend the rest of the event promoting her business.

During the wedding breakfast, Sophie tried to soothe a screaming toddler, entertain two bored children, and assist with moving wine bottles from tables of non-drinkers onto tables of those who liked a tipple. Clare made a beeline for the venue manager. She could see trouble brewing about the Manolo Blahnik shoe and needed to advise that it wasn't the venue's responsibility. There were signs for the general public not to use the stage. The manager listened politely. Clare was the most attractive Wedding Planner's Assistant he'd ever met. Come to think of it, he hadn't known a Wedding Planner to be accompanied by assistants before. *Weddings by Saffronella* must be a well-established business. He'd recommend it to future clients; he wouldn't mind meeting Clare again.

Saffie assessed the room before handing out her business cards. She could tell which couples weren't married and which needed to take the plunge. She waited until after the speeches and was about to walk across the empty dancefloor when she received a firm hand on her shoulder. 'It's Saffronella, isn't it? Now, tell me why you turned down my wife's request of assistance at our daughter's wedding.'

Saffie stared at the man behind her. 'I don't know what you're talking about.'

'I'm Arthur Bloomfield. My daughter's getting married in the Maldives in two years' time and you've said you're already booked. Now, I may be getting a bit old in the tooth, but as far as I can see, your business is booming. You should be expanding rather than turning clients away. What do you have to say about that?'

Saffie gulped. 'Well, that's very kind of you to offer your advice, Mr Bloomfield.'

Arthur Bloomfield let out a massive chuckle as he nodded towards a newly-roped-off play area in the corner of the room. 'Now that's what I call going beyond the call of duty; that's one of your staff, isn't it?'

Saffie marched over to the play area and stood with hands on hips. 'Sophie! What are you doing? Where did you get that penguin's outfit from? You look ridiculous.'

Sophie's green eyes peered through the penguin's mouth. 'Laura put me in charge of the children and the guy behind the bar with the blonde hair found me this costume. It was the choice of this or a Father Christmas outfit.'

Saffie gritted her teeth. This was not how she saw her business going. She was supposed to be managing a refined event, not running a holiday camp. To make matters worse, she caught sight of Clare with the mother of the bride, who was waving her Manolo Blahnik shoe in the air. Saffie was about to rush over to see if Clare needed assistance when the venue manager touched her arm. He smiled at her and said, 'Leave this to me.'

Saffie watched as the manager produced a bouquet from behind his back and gave it to Laura's blushing mother in return for the broken shoe. He turned and walked back towards Saffie. 'It was Clare's idea. The bride's mother is only entitled to her own embarrassment. She was trespassing by ascending onto the stage. Clare said it would be a nice token to clear the air with some flowers and to remove the shoe. Out of sight, out of mind.'

The Master of Ceremonies entered the room in all his splendour. Saffie checked the clock on her phone. Everything was going to plan – it was time for the bride and groom to cut the cake. That gave Saffie the chance to take a break. She picked up a glass of champagne from a tray on a table and headed up the stairs to the roof terrace. She was two steps from the top when she heard a man's voice:

'I'll bring Digby Hamilton-Smythe to the ground for gazumping me on that penthouse in the West End. I'd promised it to Eloise and Rufus as a wedding present. The deal was all but done when he turned up with a cash offer.'

Another man responded: 'Well, count me in on bringing old Digby down. We don't need to play by the book. He played dirty by tripping me up at the start of the 100 metres at Eton. He blamed it on my shoelace.'

'How could he blame it on a shoelace? Weren't you in the blocks?'

'It was before I got to the blocks.'

'I see. Well, it's about time Digby's good fortune changed.'

'Exactly!'

The first man continued to gossip. 'Have you met Digby's daughter? She's a waste of space, that one. Apparently, he's buying the penthouse for her. There's no chance of her settling down with a decent job. At least when she's got her own property, she'll be a better catch for a prospective husband.'

The second man coughed. 'Well, Jamie had a lucky escape – he went out with her. We were so thankful when he dumped her for Laura.'

The first man laughed. 'So you know Saffronella then? I arranged for my wife to scare her off our daughter's wedding. We gave her a list of criteria that was so far from the truth she ran a mile.'

The second man clapped his hands. 'Good on you! Those Hamilton-Smythes need knocking down a peg or two. Have you seen the time? We should get back downstairs before our wives send out a search party.'

5

DO OR DIE

Saffie was in shock – she didn't know what to do. She could run, or she could tackle the bullies head-on. She put the glass of champagne down on a window ledge in the stairwell and headed onto the roof terrace.

'Mr Bloomfield and Mr Coolridge, what a fascinating conversation you are having. There's no need to waste your time trying to bring my father down, as I am witness to your plotting.' Saffie turned her attention to Arthur Bloomfield. 'I will call my father this evening and ask him to cancel his offer on the penthouse. I will be buying my own soon enough.'

Saffie glanced over her shoulder as she turned to head back down the stairs. 'Oh, and Mr Coolridge, *I* dumped your son.'

Remembering to pick up the glass of champagne, Saffie downed it in two. She steadied herself before walking down the remainder of the steps. Never before had she been more determined to make a go of things. She caught sight of the waitress who had lent her the dress and went over to thank her. 'Thank you so much for lending me this. I didn't catch your name.'

'Oh, it's Rebecca.'

Saffie smiled. 'This is such a lovely dress to keep in your locker.'

Rebecca lowered her eyes. 'Yes, it is. I was wearing it on New Year's Eve.'

'Oh, I see, staff party?'

'No. I was meeting my boyfriend in a restaurant over the road. I thought he was going to propose, but he didn't turn up. I came over here, dumped the dress, and went home in my uniform. That dress is unlucky. I'll take it to a charity shop after tonight.'

Saffie shivered. That was strange as she wasn't superstitious. She did feel a bit uncomfortable, though. She felt like she was being watched. Saffie turned and headed towards the bar – she *was* being watched! The videographer wasn't just *watching* her; he was *filming* her. Saffie was furious and, as she stepped out of shot, she noticed the camera was focused on a small group of people huddled around a table. She'd no doubt receive more of the annoying man's wrath for getting in the way again. She held her breath as he walked over to speak to her.

'You look great in that dress. Will you be wearing it to other weddings? We're bound to bump into one another again. Two of my future clients are here tonight, and I've recommended your services. Here's my card so that you can recommend me to *your* clients too.'

With that, the videographer walked off to take footage of the bride and groom's first dance. Saffie read the name on the card: *Benjamin Brooker – Videographer Extraordinaire.*

Saffie scoffed. "Extraordinaire"! So Benjamin Brooker thought he was "Remarkable, Superb, Excellent", or such like. What a big-headed oaf. If it weren't for him, she'd still be wearing her white dress. Now, there was a thought. She should send him the cleaning bill.

With most of the children headed off to their beds or sleeping in their parents' arms, Sophie was able to join Clare on the roof terrace. 'I think our jobs are done for the day. Shall we ask Saffie if we can be excused? I'm worn out after all that childminding.'

Clare was thoughtful. 'I think Saffie's onto a good thing here. Had we known about the requirement for childminding, we could have worked it into the costs.'

'Laura did *ask* me to do it. I didn't volunteer.'

'Well then, we'll invoice Jamie as an "added extra". Now that we've done one wedding, albeit we came in at a late stage, I have a good awareness of how we should handle the finances.'

Sophie laughed. 'I should hope so. You *are* qualified! My business mind has been kicking in too. Marketing is the key. We could hold a promotional event at Saffie's office.'

Clare rubbed her hands together. 'Great idea! We should aim for something soon. Summer's the perfect time to host an event. We can hold it in the gardens.'

Saffie couldn't resist having another word with Rebecca. 'Are Wedding Planners the norm at weddings here?'

Rebecca frowned. 'There are a few. However, most brides are good at organising their own weddings.'

'Do you think I could make a go of being a Wedding Planner? This is my first event.'

Rebecca smiled. 'I think you and your team would be in demand. Sophie is brilliant with children and at noticing when the guests require anything, and Clare is good with disputes.'

It was now Saffie's turn to frown. 'Shouldn't the staff at the venue do everything that Sophie and Clare have been doing?'

Rebecca laughed. 'To a degree, yes, but not with such a personal touch. Why don't you have a word with Heinrich? I can tell he's impressed with your team.'

'Who's Heinrich?'

'You've just failed the most crucial thing in business: Establish names and remember them. Heinrich is the venue manager.'

'Who taught you that?'

'No one. It's obvious.'

Saffie hugged Rebecca. 'Thank you, Rebecca. You've helped me so much. I'll return your dress before I leave.'

Rebecca smiled. 'Well, I still have yours in a bag, so at least you'll have something to go home in.'

Heinrich was tall. His glasses framed his large brown eyes, and his short dark hair was styled to perfection. Saffie took a deep breath as she looked up at him. 'I don't suppose you could give me some informal feedback on how my team performed today, could you?'

Heinrich nodded. 'Of course. Your team was very professional. I will recommend your services.'

Saffie could have kissed him but limited her excitement to a blush. 'That's very kind of you. It was our first wedding. I need all the help I can get to make this work.'

Saffie checked the time. She needed to call her father before he boarded a flight to Los Angeles. 'Hi, Daddy! I have something important to tell you. You must listen carefully, as I have never been so serious about anything in my life . . .'

6

START-UP PLAN

The following day Saffie summoned Clare and Sophie to her office. She sat on the marble desk while her friends were seated in the gold brocade dining room chairs.

'I need you both to hand your notices in tomorrow. You're too talented to be wasted in boring office jobs when you could be working full-time for me.'

Clare laughed. 'You couldn't afford us.'

Saffie smiled. 'Oh, yes, I can. I've had a long discussion with my father which resulted in him saving a fortune, well the cost of a penthouse in the West End to be precise.'

Clare whistled. 'A penthouse in the West End? That's right; your father's saved a fortune.'

Saffie continued, 'Well, he's decided to put his money to better use by investing in my business. I will, of course, pay him back over time, but for me to have any chance of getting off the ground, I need to go all out and go big.'

Sophie could hear Digby Hamilton-Smythe saying those very words. 'OK . . . so how does that affect us?'

'My father will cover the cost of your salaries for the first year. He'll review the situation after that. It just means that we need to put all our effort into making the business successful.'

Sophie winced. 'It's a risk. What if we aren't successful? We'll be out of jobs.'

Saffie held her shoulders back. 'I have every intention of making a success of this. I know we can do it. And, yes, it is a risk for you both; my father is aware of that. He's prepared to pay your current salaries, plus ten per cent. He's even suggesting a bonus scheme. Of course, Clare could establish a proposal for that.'

Clare stared at Sophie, who was trying not to smile. 'Well, I've been awake half the night considering a financial planning model. It would look good on my CV to highlight I was a key player in a business start-up.'

Sophie clapped her hands. 'Well, count me in! I have lots of ideas of how to promote the business.

Clare and I spoke yesterday about holding an event here in the gardens; it's the perfect time of year. We could invite potential clients and wedding suppliers too – it's good to network.'

Saffie's thoughts turned to Benjamin Brooker. If she had to see him again for the sake of her business, then she'd have to suffer it. 'What about you, Clare? Please tell me you'll be our Financial Controller.'

This opportunity wasn't too much of a risk for Clare. She'd already been looking around for an exciting challenge, and she could see the potential in this one. She held out her hand to shake Saffie's. 'Of course. I just hope this venture doesn't damage our friendship. Financial Controllers are pretty strict – I'll be counting every penny.'

Saffie slid off the desk. 'Enough said; I'll pop into the house to find a bottle of champagne before we start. My father can pay for that!'

*

By four-thirty in the afternoon, the champagne remained unopened. The summer house was littered with designs, lists, financial projections, and a catalogue of items to purchase – with office seating being at the top.

Sophie rubbed her forehead. 'Are we agreed then that Clare will have a window desk overlooking the lake and I'll have a swimming pool view?'

34

Clare looked up from her calculations. 'I'll sit anywhere. I won't have time to look out of the window if our projections are correct.'

Saffie's phone rang, and she answered it. 'Hello, it's Saffronella speaking … Oh, Mr Bloomfield … Yes, that's right, I spoke to my father … I'm so pleased you're now purchasing the apartment for Eloise, who is marrying Rufus. What? My father has recommended me as their Wedding Planner … November this year … that's a bit different from the Maldives in two years' time … No, no, no, of course I can fit them in. That's no trouble at all. What's that? They've done most of the work already. How lovely.'

Clare and Sophie were both making thumbs-up signs and forcing exaggerated smiles. Sophie pointed to a mock-up of an advertisement for the promotional event. Saffie winked before continuing, 'Well, it would be great to see Eloise and Rufus at our Wedding Planning Extravaganza on Sunday the 4th of August. We can have a catch up then … Where? … It'll be in the grounds of our Head Office in Kensington. We'll be sending out invitations via email as it's short notice. Can you please advise the best email address for your daughter?'

Saffie ended the call, and Clare popped open the champagne. 'Beggars can't be choosers. Good on your father to get us a wedding as part of his apartment deal. We'll have to pick up scraps the first year. Most people plan weddings a year or two in advance. At least we'll know our stuff before we go for the big guns.'

The girls clinked glasses, and Sophie stared at Clare. 'Who are the big guns?'

'Celebrities, royalty, those with yachts. The list is endless.'

Saffie sipped her champagne. The warm feeling she felt at this exciting time was tempered by annoyance. She'd emailed Benjamin Brooker last night requesting confirmation he'd pay for her dry cleaning bill. The irritating man hadn't bothered to respond. Of course, he may be at another wedding, but that was no excuse to ignore her for nearly a day.

Sophie screeched in delight. 'Peacocks! You've got peacocks! We must get those in the promotional shots.'

Clare raised an eyebrow. 'Why? We're not holding weddings here.'

Sophie held a hand to her chest. 'I think you may have just come up with a brilliant idea. Some people want small events. They get married in a registry office on their own with a couple of witnesses then recreate the wedding experience in a beautiful setting with just a few guests. We could offer that as a niche service.' Sophie looked at Saffie. 'That's if your parents would approve.'

Saffie shrugged. 'My parents will approve of anything for me to get a career off the ground.'

Clare noted the potential new business

opportunity before leaning back in her chair. 'In that case, I suggest we order pizzas all round.'

7

PROMOTIONAL EVENT

Clare sat in the summer house, updating her spreadsheets. The cost of the catering team had shot up with Saffie's last-minute request for a hog roast beside the swimming pool. Her reasoning for the extra expense to Clare was that the weather was too good to miss such an opportunity. Clare turned the ceiling fan up a notch. Saffie had insisted they all wear their uniforms today, albeit Clare and Sophie could leave their jackets off as it was so warm. Clare glanced out of the window at Saffie in her element. She looked as cool as a cucumber in her short white skater dress. The cost of a new dress would also need to be added to the spreadsheet – the wine stain hadn't come out of the first one.

Sophie entered the summer house carrying two diet cokes. 'Wow! It's much cooler in here. I can't believe we have to wear long-sleeved blouses and trousers on such a hot day. Saffie's all right, of course. Let's put a proposal together outlining the benefits of us wearing shorts.'

Clare sipped her drink. 'I prefer to look business-like. It's swings and roundabouts anyway. Saffie will be cold at winter weddings.'

Sophie raised her eyes. 'Not when she's bought a white fur coat.'

Clare raised her eyes too. 'Now, enough about our uniform, what's the latest take-up on the guestlist for today?'

Sophie glanced at her iPad. 'Sixty-three acceptances at the last count . . . oh, no, make that sixty-four – Ben has managed to move his diary around to get here.'

'Ben? You don't mean Benjamin Brooker?'

'Yes, I do. Saffie's going to be astonished.'

'Astonished? Annoyed more like it. He's not returned any of her emails or phone messages about her dress. He's ignored her.'

'I know. Ben's been quick to respond to *me*, though.'

Clare raised an eyebrow. 'I wonder what he's up to?'

Sophie winked. 'I think it's a classic case of "treat them mean, keep them keen". I saw him watching her at Jamie and Laura's wedding.'

'Are you going to tell her he's coming this afternoon?'

Sophie grinned. 'No. Saffie can have a nice surprise.'

*

By two-thirty, most of the guests had arrived. Sophie had provided them with welcome packs while Clare watched the proceedings from the coolness of the summer house – someone had to keep a check on emails and be there to take any potential bookings that arose from today's event.

It was after three o'clock when Clare saw him striding around the lake. Benjamin Brooker wore jeans and a white shirt. His unruly brown hair framed a strong, tanned face. Clare wondered what colour his eyes were beneath his designer sunglasses. He headed towards the swimming pool where most guests had assembled for the hog roast. Saffie's short white dress made her stand out from the crowd, and before long, the *Videographer Extraordinaire* was standing behind her.

Sophie bounded into the summer house carrying a large box. 'Ben's here! He asked me to give this to Saffie after the event.'

Clare's eyes widened. 'Shall we look inside? We wouldn't want our boss to break a fingernail if the elusive Benjamin Brooker has planted a mouse-trap in there. He seems intent on keeping her on her toes.'

Sophie shook her head. 'We shouldn't. Should we?'

Clare untied the white ribbon and lifted the lid of the pink box. She closed one eye. 'There's a card inside. I'm trying not to read it, but it's not in an envelope.'

Sophie picked the card up and read it aloud:

> *I couldn't let this dress go to a charity shop; you look too good in it. Meet me at seven o'clock tonight outside the entrance to the Tower of London. Make sure you wear the dress. BB*

The girls swooned before putting the card back and tying up the box. Sophie did a little jig on the spot before announcing: 'I'm going over to the pool area. When Saffie sees Ben, she'll be in shock. I should have warned her he was coming.'

Clare gasped. 'Too late, she knows he's here. He's just saved her from a fate worse than death.'

Sophie joined Clare at the window. 'What happened?'

'He caught her before she fell into the pool.'

'How did she nearly fall into the pool?'

'I could swear that woman in the red dress intentionally bumped into her.'

'That's Eloise Bloomfield.'

'No surprise there then. A bride who's been forced to use our services.'

Saffie wriggled free of the strong arm encompassing her waist. 'It's you! Why did you bump into me?!'

Benjamin Brooker removed his sunglasses and held his hands in the air. 'Not guilty, this time.'

Saffie noticed he was more tanned than a month ago. It brought out the colour of his cerulean blue eyes. 'Have you been away? I've been trying to get hold of you.'

'I was on a work trip in the South of France.'

'Well, you owe me the cost of this dress. The one covered in red wine didn't survive the dry cleaners.'

Ben smiled at Saffie. 'You know my preferred dress.'

Saffie frowned. 'The silver one? Well, that's unlucky, and it's now in a charity shop.'

Ben replaced his sunglasses and turned to leave. 'Until next time.'

Saffie stamped her foot – that man was so annoying. It was pointless wasting time on him. She needed to make the most of today's event. Only two potential weddings so far – she needed more.

Two hours later, Saffie shook hands with the last of the guests and headed towards the summer house. She walked with a spring in her step. She couldn't wait to catch up with Clare and Sophie to establish the take-up of their services.

Clare was printing a list when Saffie strode in. 'Here you go. Four weddings signed up, six potentials, and a whole raft of suppliers who want to work with us.'

Saffie scanned the document. 'Benjamin Brooker's not on here. I take it he doesn't want anything to do with us.'

Clare glared at Sophie, who reached under her desk for the box before speaking, 'We didn't get a chance to ask him. He didn't stay long enough – but he did bring this for you.'

Saffie was well aware the annoying man hadn't stayed for long. Why had he brought her a box? She tore off the white ribbon and lifted the lid before reading the card. Sophie and Clare waited with bated breath. Saffie shoved the card back in the box and replaced the lid before heading towards the door with it.

Sophie called out: 'What's in the box? What does the card say?'

Saffie glanced over her shoulder. 'Oh, he's just brought me some still shots of his work. I'll have a look through when I've got time. I forgot to mention; I have a hot date tonight. I need to get ready for it. Just lock up when you've finished. Thanks for all your help today.'

Saffie closed the office door, and Clare raised her eyebrows at Sophie. 'Are you thinking what I'm thinking?'

Sophie smiled. 'Definitely. I'll meet you in the coffee shop outside the Tower of London at six-forty-five. This is going to be too good to miss!'

8

A HOT DATE

Saffie couldn't remember when she'd been so excited about going on a date. Her annoyance with Benjamin Brooker had dispersed as soon as she'd opened that box and read the card. An image of his cerulean blue eyes flashed through her mind, and a warm feeling encompassed her. No – she'd forgiven him for ignoring her earlier than that. He'd been there when she'd nearly fallen into the pool this afternoon. She could still feel the strength of his arm around her waist and smell the freshness of his aftershave.

Sophie waved to Clare through the coffee shop window. Clare waved back. She'd bought Sophie a latte; she knew there was no way her friend would be late to watch the "show". They had a perfect view of the entrance to the Tower of London from there.

At six fifty-five, Benjamin Brooker walked past the coffee shop and went to stand across the road. He was wearing a black suit and an open-necked white shirt. Sophie reached over and squeezed Clare's hand. 'This is so exciting; he's bought her pink roses!'

At six fifty-eight, two men approached Ben, and he dropped his head before following them. Sophie was shocked. 'Saffie will be here in a minute! Wait here and look out for her. Ben's going to be late!' Sophie rushed out of the coffee shop to establish what Ben was up to. Clare ordered another cappuccino. She guessed Saffie would arrive between seven-fifteen to seven-thirty. She wouldn't want to appear keen.

The two men led Ben to a motorboat on the Thames. He followed without protest. Sophie waved her arms in the air as he turned to get on the boat. Although there was some distance, she could see Ben's eyes light up. He left the roses on the quayside and reached inside his jacket pocket for a notepad and pen. Sophie saw him scribble something and tuck it under the flowers. The motorboat sped off.

Sophie had never run so fast in her life. What on earth was going on? She picked up the flowers and read the note:

> *These are for Saffronella. Don't tell*
> *her you saw me. Our secret. BB*

It was now seven-twelve. Sophie rushed back to the coffee shop with the flowers and note, which she held out to Clare. 'Look at this.'

Clare read the note. 'He said to keep it secret.'

Sophie rolled her eyes. 'This is too big for me to keep to myself. You're in my circle of trust.'

Clare pulled at her bottom lip. 'I understand. We can't tell Saffie, though.'

Sophie glared at Clare. 'We definitely cannot.'

Clare glanced out of the window. 'It's seven-twenty now, and she's walking along outside. What should we do?'

Sophie's heart sank. 'We need to keep a low profile and go home. She won't wait around for too long.'

Clare stood up. 'I'm not feeling great about this, but you're right. Let's get out of here before she sees us.'

Saffie stood outside the Tower of London and checked her watch. Seven-twenty-two. What a loser! He couldn't even wait around for twenty minutes. Was she not worth it? Well, she wasn't going to wait a minute longer. Another thought crossed her mind – was the dress unlucky, had she been stood up? Saffie made up her mind there and then. There was no better place for the dress than the charity shop. And as far as

Benjamin Brooker was concerned, he would never be her videographer of choice. She wished with all her heart their paths never crossed again.

*

The following morning, Sophie peered inside the paper carrier bag on her desk. There was a note from Saffie:

Please take this to the charity shop
on your way home. Love Saffie x

Clare's shoulders slumped. 'I'm not feeling good about all of this. It's the dress, isn't it?'

Sophie nodded before pushing the bag beneath her desk. 'What would Digby Hamilton-Smythe say?'

Clare sighed. 'Keep calm and carry on.'

Sophie forced a smile. 'Exactly. He's our investor. We have his daughter's best interests at heart, and we need to draw a line under our nosiness. If we hadn't broken into the box and spied on Saffie, we'd be none the wiser.'

Clare cringed before swivelling around in her chair to see Saffie walking around the lake. She took a deep breath and waited for her to enter the office.

Sophie was the first to speak: 'How did your hot date go last night?'

Saffie shrugged. 'I was too whacked after the promotional event to go. I can't believe how much that took out of me. I had a hot bath and an early night. I'm raring to go this morning. I can't believe how well we're doing! What do we need to focus on first?'

Clare's heart sank for her friend, but she needed to hold it together. 'A wedding on a yacht in September.'

Saffie gasped. 'A yacht? Where in the world?'

Sophie responded: 'Majorca. Sorry it's not more exotic. The couple's wedding planner has pulled out, and we have six weeks to pick up the pieces.'

Saffie's stomach churned. 'Do they have a videographer booked?'

Clare swivelled round in her chair. 'They certainly do. *Dream Movies by Dean* is their supplier of choice.'

Saffie felt a massive sense of relief. 'Well, I expect you both to attend the wedding with me. There'll be more hazards on a yacht than just unruly children. By the way, why is there a vase of pink roses on my desk?'

Sophie shrugged her shoulders. 'They're just a gift because you are so amazing.'

Saffie hugged her friends. 'Thanks, girls. I couldn't do this without you.'

9

WELCOME TO MAJORCA

The girls climbed into a chauffeur-driven car at Palma airport – they couldn't believe their luck. An all-expenses-paid week away in the sunshine. OK – they had to work for the privilege. Hen and Stag Do's on Monday night preceded three days of excursions for the guests before the wedding on Friday.

On arrival at their hotel overlooking the marina, the trio headed to their rooms. Clare and Sophie were sharing, and Saffie had the room next door. She walked along the corridor while taking a call from the bride. 'Yes, we've just arrived … Is he really? … That will be nice … Of course we'll look after him … We'll see you in the morning.'

Clare and Sophie stood outside their room, waiting for an update on the conversation. Saffie called down the corridor. 'The videographer is staying here too. We're invited to join the bride and groom on the yacht in the morning. Let's get unpacked and meet downstairs in the bar in half an hour. We can have a drink before dinner. See you soon.'

Sophie lifted her suitcase onto her bed and sat down to search for *Dream Movies by Dean* on her phone. As far as she could make out, it was a one-person business. She let out a gasp before turning to Clare. 'Guess what the videographer's name is?'

Clare raised her eyes to the ceiling. 'Dean.'

Sophie raised her eyebrows. 'Dean Brooker. You don't think . . .?'

'That they're related?'

'Well?'

Clare laughed. 'It would be a mighty big coincidence if they were. Is there a photograph on that website?'

Sophie brought up an image on her phone. 'They look nothing alike. Dean's not so hard-looking. He's got softer features. It might be the blonde hair. No – wait a minute – it's the laughter lines around his eyes.'

Clare stifled a snigger. 'And what colour are those eyes?'

'An unusual shade of green with tiny gold flecks. No – they're not related. I can tell already that Dean will be a dream to have around.'

*

The following morning, Saffie and her team joined Anastasia and Ross on their yacht for breakfast. Saffie held out her hand. 'It's so nice to finally meet you both, I'm Saffronella, and my colleagues are Clare and Sophie. I believe you've all spoken.'

Anastasia pulled her brown curls into a loose bun which she fastened with a shell adorned clip. 'We certainly have. I feel I know you all already. You've been a godsend over the last six weeks. First, our wedding planner pulls out, then the videographer. All we need now is for the florist to come down with an extreme case of hay fever on Thursday when she's booked to decorate the boat.' Anastasia tutted. 'Such a pretty girl that wedding planner, she was Spanish and had promised to perform a flamenco at my Hen Do.'

Saffie's mind was racing. 'Your videographer pulled out?'

Ross leant back in his chair. 'Yes. That was a disappointment – I've known Ben Brooker for years. Still, he didn't leave us in the lurch; he's sent his brother instead. Have you met Dean yet?'

The girls sat open-mouthed as the interior doors of

52

the yacht opened, and a tall, blonde, smiley man walked onto the deck carrying a coffee. 'Well, hello everyone. Ben has told me all about you. I just nipped inside to get a drink, my flight got in late last night, and I'm desperately in need of caffeine.'

*

Back at the hotel, Sophie and Clare tried to piece the chain of events together. Sophie paced around their bedroom. 'I don't care what Saffie says, Ben didn't run off with the Spanish wedding planner; he was kidnapped and bundled onto a speedboat on the Thames.'

Clare rubbed her forehead. 'You're exaggerating. You know as well as I do that he willingly followed two men onto that boat.'

Sophie fell backwards onto the bed. 'I don't like this. I don't like it at all!'

Clare closed the lid of her laptop. 'Come on. We need to be at the nightclub in half an hour. Make sure you bring the list Anastasia gave you for the Hen Do tomorrow night.'

*

Saffie was still on the yacht. She'd had a meeting with the captain about the ceremony on Friday; she'd spoken to the crew about the timetable for the week;

and she'd checked the chef had been advised of all dietary requirements. Most of the guests would be arriving that afternoon, with the remaining two couples flying in tomorrow morning. She sat at the bar in the lounge and updated the schedule on her laptop. A fresh cup of latte appeared next to her. 'Would you like anything to go in that – a drop of brandy perhaps?'

Dean's green eyes twinkled, and Saffie glanced around the room before whispering, 'Don't you think you're making yourself too at home? You should ask permission before strutting around like you own the place?'

Dean shrugged. 'I'm a chilled out person who's perfectly capable of making a cup of coffee for a friend. Servants aren't my thing.'

Saffie cringed. 'You *will* behave this week, won't you? Technically, I'm your manager. *Weddings by Saffronella* is the umbrella business, and we'll be paying your fee. We're a one-stop-shop, a stress-free service for the happy couple. If there's any problem with you, then the buck falls with me.'

Dean pulled out the barstool next to Saffie and sat down. 'Is that so? Well, there *is* a little problem I've identified, and I'm delighted I now have someone to share it with.'

Saffie sighed. 'What's the problem?'

'The umbrella company hasn't booked a photographer.'

Saffie scoffed. 'You're the photographer.'

Dean shook his head. 'I'm the videographer. I don't do both.'

Saffie thought back to Laura and Jamie's wedding. Ben was the videographer; there was a photographer too. She gulped. 'Well, we've had to pick up the pieces from the Spanish wedding planner who ran off at the same time as your brother. There's been no mention of the requirement of a photographer. It's a small wedding; can't you do both on this occasion?'

Dean shook his head again. 'I'm not Superman. I may have a solution, though.'

'What's that?'

'I was speaking to Sophie earlier, and she showed me some shots she'd taken on her phone; she has an eye for detail. I could work with Sophie.'

Saffie cringed. 'That's not professional. I'll sort something out by Friday. Just leave it with me.' She drank the latte and made a quick exit. What was it with videographers? Why were they all so annoying?

10

A SURPRISE ENCOUNTER

The nightclub was packed. Anastasia and her friends edged their way around the dancefloor to where Saffie and Clare were waiting in a private alcove with balloons, bottles of champagne, and canapés. Anastasia squealed with delight. 'My last night of freedom! Keep the drinks flowing!'

Sophie had offered to join the Stag Do in the sports bar over the road. *Weddings by Saffronella* needed to be represented at all times this week, besides Ross had asked Dean to join them, and Sophie felt he might be a bit left out without knowing anyone. Dean sat on a stool next to her while Ross clowned around with his mates as they recalled racy stories of their rugby days. After two rounds of drinks, Dean grabbed hold of Sophie's hand and whispered in her ear, 'That's enough obscenity in front of a lady. Let's find somewhere else to go. No one will miss us.'

Meanwhile, back at the nightclub, a waiter handed Saffie an envelope. She looked over at Clare, who was busy chatting to the maid of honour. Saffie opened the envelope, but it was far too dark to read the handwritten message, so she decided to make her way outside.

The fresh air and dusky light that greeted her made a welcome change from two hours of rubbing shoulders with strangers in a basement. The drone of thudding music gave way to the sound of crickets, and Saffie sat down on a bench to read her note. She was soon joined by a man. His leg touched hers, and she screamed.

'Don't scream. It's me! I asked the waiter to give you the note. I didn't think you'd join me so quickly.'

Saffie recognised the voice, and she turned to look into his cerulean blue eyes. 'What are you doing here?'

Ben sighed. 'It's a long story.'

'You stood me up outside the Tower of London.'

'I didn't. Trust me. Well, I didn't plan to, anyway. I was there by seven o'clock, but I needed to leave soon after that.'

'I don't believe you.'

'Ask Sophie.'

'What?!'

Ben took hold of Saffie's hand. 'Come with me. I'm celebrating.'

'Celebrating what?'

'My freedom.'

*

Clare glanced around the room. Saffie was missing. She hadn't seen her for half an hour. She was about to search the building when a waiter tapped her on the shoulder. 'Your friend has a sore head, as you call it. She go home.'

Clare sighed, both out of relief and annoyance. It was up to *her* now to get the bride and her guests back on the yacht in one piece. She didn't envy Sophie having to do the same with the men.

*

The tapas bar was cosy, and Ben ordered a selection of nibbles to go with a bottle of champagne. Saffie didn't think she could eat a thing. 'Have you called it off with the Spanish wedding planner?'

Ben laughed. 'What?! Oh, I see, *that's* what you thought. You sound jealous.'

Saffie shrugged. 'Not at all. I can tell you're the type of man who gets what he wants. It's too much of a coincidence you both disappeared at the same time.'

Ben shook his head. 'You couldn't be further from the truth. The trouble I've been in is partially your fault. When I was filming you at Jamie and Laura's wedding in July, I captured some footage I was obliged to hand over to the police. All hell broke loose after that. I was told to lie low and given police protection.'

Saffie leant forward and grabbed Ben's hand. 'Are you OK?'

'I'm fine. All arrests have been made now, and the footage I provided will remain anonymous. I'm risking a lot by telling you this much, but I needed to explain my erratic behaviour. Do you forgive me for neglecting you? I want us to start off on a good footing.'

Saffie's heart leapt, and she squeezed Ben's hand. 'There's nothing to forgive, and don't worry, I won't mention a word of what you've just told me to anyone. I've forgotten about it already.' Her appetite had returned, and she munched on an olive. She still had a pressing question to ask: 'How does Sophie know you didn't stand me up outside the Tower of London?'

Ben smiled. 'It was a total coincidence and an extreme chance of luck. When the protection team came to take me away by motorboat, I saw her in the distance. I caught her eye, and she saw me leave the flowers on the quayside. I scribbled a note, so she knew they were for you.'

Saffie's mind turned to the vase of pink roses on her desk. Why hadn't Sophie told her they were from Ben? Ben read her thoughts. 'Don't be cross with Sophie. I swore her to secrecy. Now, let's draw a line under the past and discuss the future. What are your plans for this week? Is there any chance we can meet up when you're not working?'

Saffie nibbled on a triangle of Manchego cheese while she considered her answer. 'We've got a packed schedule for the next three days. Wine tasting and lunch at a vineyard tomorrow. Scuba diving and beach barbecue on Wednesday. On Thursday there's shopping, followed by a hot air balloon ride. The wedding's scheduled for two o'clock on Friday on the yacht. We're on duty the whole time we're here.'

'Wow! It sounds like your team has been busy arranging all of that. You won't have time to come up for air.'

Saffie wiped her mouth on a serviette. 'Of course, we could always make room for an extra guest. Especially one who's good with a camera. Anastasia and Ross will be delighted you're here.'

Ben blushed before the sound of laughter and

scurrying of bodies drew his attention to the scene outside. He opened his wallet and took out a wad of Euros which he handed to a passing waiter.

Ben took hold of Saffie's hand. 'We need to go. I've known Ross for years, and I can tell when he's going to throw up. Why on earth people strap their best friends to lampposts before their wedding is beyond me. We need to get him back to my boat.'

Saffie frowned. '*Your* boat?'

Ben shrugged. 'I said they could use it for the week as a wedding present. I've booked a room at the same hotel as Dean.'

Saffie's eyes lit up. 'Really? We're staying there too.'

Ben winked. 'Another happy coincidence – that means we can have breakfast together.'

11

A BUSY WEEK

Saffie was annoyed with Sophie in more ways than one. Apart from keeping secrets from her, how could she let the Stag Do go unsupervised? At least Clare had been professional enough to ensure Anastasia returned to the boat in a respectable state and at a reasonable time. Ross, on the other hand, was missing a pair of designer jeans and nursing a hangover so bad he'd backed out of today's excursion.

Sophie was defiant when Saffie confronted her. 'A Stag Do is no place for a lady. I suffered the first two hours but had an early night after that to recover from the trauma ... What do you mean about not telling you that you weren't stood up outside the Tower of London? We – I mean I – didn't know you were supposed to be at the Tower of London. You said you'd had a bath and gone to bed after the promotional event … It was lucky I saw Ben leave the flowers on the quayside. I didn't tell you they were from him because he asked me not to. So, really Saffie, I can't see your problem.'

Clare stepped in to diffuse the situation before Sophie said something she shouldn't. 'Stop arguing, you two. We have a business to run. The minibus is leaving for the vineyard in fifteen minutes, and we need to be there before the guests.'

Sophie wasn't finished. 'How do you know I saw Ben outside the Tower of London? Have you heard from him?'

Saffie blushed. 'He turned up last night. Not only did he turn up, but he also announced that he owns the yacht. Now I know why his brother has been making himself at home on it. You'll see him soon enough. I've checked with Anastasia, and he'll be attending the wedding as a guest; he'll also be taking some still shots as his brother is incapable of doing both.'

Sophie narrowed her eyes. 'Dean isn't incapable of anything.'

Clare looked from one friend to the other. They both glowed this morning. So, Sophie had left the Stag Do early with Dean, and Saffie had left Clare in the lurch to spend the evening with Ben. Her stomach sank, with two team members distracted, this was going to be a long week.

*

Anastasia was annoyed her groom couldn't get out of bed this morning. She had a headache, but at least she'd made an effort to join their guests at the vineyard. She was thrilled the attractive Ben Brooker had moved his diary around to get to Majorca in time for the wedding. It was a bonus having Dean there too. Who needed a hungover Ross when two handsome brothers were on the loose? Anastasia patted the chair next to her. 'Ben! Come and join me in the absence of my husband-to-be. Is there anything I should know about him before we take the plunge on Friday? I also want to know why you're single; it's such a waste.'

Sophie giggled and whispered in Dean's ear, 'Did you capture that on video?'

Dean raised his eyebrows. 'No! I want a happy bride and groom on Friday. It's just a shame I've got to work all this week, and Ben gets to be a guest.'

Sophie smiled. 'Ben's lined up to take the photographs on the wedding day, so he'll support you then.'

Dean laughed. 'Support me! That'll be a first. My brother has always been destined for bigger and better things. Still, I expect he'll "suffer" supporting me if it helps Saffie out. He's got the hots for her.'

Sophie glanced at Saffie, who was leaning over Ben with a bowl of roasted almonds. She saw Ben's stunning blue eyes twinkle before his phone beeped, and he read the message on the screen. He turned to Anastasia. 'Please excuse me for a moment. I need to make an urgent call. I won't be long.' Ben stood up and smiled at Saffie before he strode across the terrace and down the steps to the car park. Sophie frowned. Whatever the call was about, Ben didn't want to be overheard.

Dean put his video camera down. 'That was rude of my brother. He always puts business first. On the other hand, I am always on the lookout for opportunities to have fun. I'll pop over and have a quiet word with Anastasia to ask if I can join in the scuba diving tomorrow. Do you want a go too?'

Sophie blushed. 'You can't do that. It's not professional; we're supposed to be working.'

Dean winked. 'Just leave it to me.'

Saffie leant over the low wall encircling the terrace to see Ben running back up the steps. He caught sight of her when he reached the top. Saffie froze as he headed straight towards her. 'We need to make the most of this week. Any chance you can escape tomorrow's activities? If so, we can drive down the coast to a small, secluded beach. There's a tapas bar nearby where we can have a leisurely lunch.'

Saffie's heart leapt. 'What should I bring?'

Ben grinned. 'A bikini would be great.'

Dean hugged Anastasia and made his way back to Sophie. 'It's all sorted. We're going scuba diving tomorrow, and Anastasia insists we go on the balloon ride on Thursday too.'

Sophie did a little clap. 'How did you manage that?'

Dean shrugged. 'Just put it down to my boyish charm.'

*

The following day couldn't come quick enough for Saffie. The drive down the coast to the secluded beach was breathtaking. Saffie didn't feel guilty about leaving Clare in charge today; she was more than capable of covering for Saffie in moments of need. Saffie was, however, annoyed with Sophie. How could she be led astray by Dean? They were supposed to be working this week, not having fun.

After a morning of swimming and sunbathing, Saffie had an appetite for lunch. She tied a sarong around her waist and took hold of Ben's hand as they headed for the tapas bar. Ben glanced down at her. 'You've certainly led a varied life so far. I think you've mentioned six failed jobs, and you're only twenty-five.' Saffie laughed. 'It's seven, actually – I need you to pay more attention.'

Ben pulled out a chair for Saffie. 'Well, my career path has been far less exciting.'

Saffie picked up a menu. 'I'm starving. What shall we order? Maybe we shouldn't overdo it as you're taking me out for dinner tonight.'

Ben raised his eyebrows. 'Am I?'

'Of course. And tomorrow night, too, after the balloon ride. Anastasia has been so kind with finding us space in one of the wicker baskets.'

Ben chuckled. 'Well, I am classed as a guest. You must be my "plus one".'

Saffie shook her head. 'No way! I'm the Wedding Planner. In fact, your brother reports to me this week. I'm the boss.'

Saffie threw an olive in her mouth before spluttering when she realised it was stuffed with a jalapeño pepper. Ben had a wry smile as he handed her a glass of water. 'Well then, Boss, I'll be led by you. You order lunch while I make a quick call. I'll be back soon.'

Ben walked across the road and strolled along the beach with his phone to his ear. Saffie huffed as she tried to read the menu, which was in Spanish. A waiter approached her. 'Ready to order, Señorita?'

Saffie placed the menu down. 'I'll be led by you. A nice variety for two people, please.'

The waiter nodded. 'A jug of sangria too?'

'That would be lovely, thank you.'

Saffie turned to stare at Ben. What was so important that it took away from the precious little time they had together? Saffie narrowed her eyes; there was something suspicious about Benjamin Brooker.

12

A CHANGE OF PLAN

By Friday morning, Clare was jaded. Saffie and Sophie had been wandering around like lovestruck teenagers and disappearing for hours on end. Neither had helped check the email account or respond to phone messages. Clare had spent every evening with a room service meal and a raft of work to catch up on. At least when they returned to London, the Brooker brothers wouldn't be on hand night and day; they'd have their own businesses to run.

A knock on the door broke Clare's thoughts. Sophie hadn't arrived back at their room until the early hours, and she was still in bed. Clare crept across the tiled floor and opened the door. She stepped into the corridor to speak with Saffie. 'Shush, Sophie's asleep.'

Saffie paced up and down. 'I have a bad feeling about the Brooker brothers.'

Clare's ears pricked up. 'Really? What makes you say that?'

'How can a videographer afford a yacht, for one thing?'

Clare tilted her head to one side as she surveyed her boss's anxiety. 'Well, I did wonder that. Is there anything else that's made you suspicious?'

Saffie nodded. 'Over the last couple of days, Ben has taken phone calls he doesn't want me to hear. He's wandered off on several occasions to speak to someone in private. There's something shady going on. When we get back to London, I'm going to keep my distance from him.'

Clare let out a sigh of relief. 'Great idea. We need to focus on our business, which is booming by the way. I've lots to update you on after today's wedding.'

Saffie hugged her friend. 'I've been a rubbish boss this week, but I'm back on track now. We need to keep Sophie focused today; at least Dean will be fully occupied with the filming. Let's make sure this wedding goes to plan. We need good references.'

Clare smiled. 'We need *great* references.'

*

Anastasia calmed her nerves with a large gin and tonic while Sophie bit her fingernails. 'It's best not to drink too much before the wedding, or you might fluff your vows.'

Anastasia waved the empty glass in the air. 'Refill, please.' Sophie took hold of the glass and filled it with tonic water and a slice of lemon. Anastasia was so stressed she wouldn't notice the difference. 'Why, oh why, did we decide to get married on a boat? Just our luck the weather's atrocious today. My mother's thrown up twice already, and my bridesmaids look like they've been dragged through a hedge backwards.'

Sophie checked the time. 'Only ten minutes until the ceremony. The rain's stopped now, and I can see a glimmer of sun poking through the clouds. Things will be perfect for you and Ross.'

Anastasia tried to stand up. 'Why's the boat still rocking then?'

Ross stood outside on the deck. Saffie adjusted the flower in his buttonhole. 'There, you look great. Just wait until you see Anastasia; she looks amazing.'

Ross fiddled with his cufflinks. 'I'm not sure this is a good idea. If the wind picks up again, the photographs and video will be ruined.'

Clare stood between Ben and Dean with a smile plastered on her face. 'There's no need to worry, Ross.

You've got two of the best men in the business on the case. They can perform miracles.' Clare coughed. 'Not that you need any miracles – I'm sure the weather will take a turn for the better.'

As a string quartet began to play, the captain went to stand beneath a blustery floral arch. That was a sign for the guests to take their seats. Saffie saw Anastasia and her father struggling down a narrow staircase, holding onto the bride's flyaway veil. She smiled at them and gave a thumbs-up sign before making a quick exit onto the quayside.

As soon as she was on solid ground, Saffie took off her shoes and ran to the hotel. By the time she got there, she was out of breath. Saffie knew the hotel manager by name. 'Oh, Rafael, I'm in desperate need of help. Can you please provide a safe place for a soon to be drenched wedding party? We only need a small room. We can salvage the catering from the boat. Please say you can help me.'

Rafael liked Saffie; she always had a ready smile for him. 'Of course. We will do our best to meet your requirements, Miss Hamilton-Smythe.'

The ceremony was over by the time Saffie got back to the yacht. She cringed at the sight of the guests clinging onto their hats as she walked over to pull Ross to one side. 'The weather is getting worse, but I've found the perfect solution. They can accommodate us at the hotel for the rest of the day. There will, of course, be a charge for room hire. Would you like me to coordinate the transfer of guests? The string quartet will sound better out of the wind too. The acoustics will be far superior.'

Ross threw an arm around Saffie. 'You're an angel. I'll let Anastasia know; we should head over there straight away.'

*

With the wedding reception underway at the hotel, Ben took the opportunity to catch up with Saffie. 'I don't know how you managed to pull this off. I'm impressed.' Saffie flashed a smile at Ben and then turned to focus on her clients.

Sophie and Clare had managed to transport the wedding cake from the boat to the hotel in one piece and felt pride in their achievement when the bride and groom cut into it. By chance, Rafael's brother was a Spanish guitar player, and as the day drew to a close, the party started.

At nine-forty-five, Rafael whispered in Saffie's ear, and she giggled. Ben was on high alert; he'd noticed the hotel manager's eyes wandering over to Saffie all day. He walked over to interrupt the camaraderie between the two but was held at arm's length by Saffie. 'Not now, Ben. Rafael has just advised me of a perfect surprise.'

Saffie stood on a chair and tapped a crystal glass with a knife. 'May I have your attention, everyone. I'm delighted to announce that today's earlier storm has passed over. My good friend, Rafael,' Saffie held an arm out to identify who she meant, and Ben edged closer to her in case she fell off the chair, 'has invited us all onto the terrace for sangria and fireworks. We need to go now as the display starts at ten o'clock.'

Ben lifted Saffie off the chair. 'How did he arrange fireworks at such short notice?'

Saffie chuckled. 'There's a fiesta across the bay from the marina. The display was cancelled due to the weather, but it's back on now. How lucky is that?'

13

BACK AT BASE

Saffie sat at her white marble desk and read the reviews on her website. 'Anastasia and Ross have been so kind; I can't believe their guests have written reviews for us too.'

Sophie giggled. 'We had so much fun in Majorca, didn't we?'

Clare scowled. Last week had been her busiest working week since she'd left university; she'd worked around the clock. There was still a backlog of emails to catch up on now they were back at base.

A buzzer sounded, and Saffie viewed the CCTV camera. 'It's Eloise Bloomfield. Does she have an appointment?'

Clare shook her head. 'No. She's scheduled to come

in with Rufus next week.'

Saffie tutted. 'OK. I'll deal with her.' She pressed the intercom button. 'Hi, Eloise. It's Saffronella. You're a week early.'

Eloise glared at the camera. 'Just let me in. I want to hear your side of the story.'

Saffie opened the gates, and Sophie winced. 'What does she mean? You haven't been anywhere near Rufus, have you?'

Saffie shrugged. 'Not that I know of.'

Eloise barged through the door of the summer house. Sophie jumped up and held out a chair for her. 'How lovely to see you. We're happy to discuss your wedding at any time you wish.'

Eloise slumped down on the chair before bursting into tears. 'What wedding? Are you having a laugh?' Saffie and Clare sat open-mouthed as Sophie handed the tearful bride a tissue. Eloise blew her nose before continuing, 'Haven't you seen the local news? Rufus and my father have been splattered all over it for days.'

Saffie leant forward on her desk. 'We've all been out of the country on an assignment. Our flight got back late last night. What's happened?'

Eloise grabbed another tissue. 'Drugs. That's what's happened. They're both part of a gang, and they were even dealing under our noses at Jamie and Laura's wedding. Was it you who told the police?'

The girls shook their heads. Sophie knelt on the floor next to Eloise and held her hand. 'We had absolutely no idea.'

Saffie was on red alert. 'No. We had no idea. How shocking for you. There were so many people at the event it could have been anyone. We were too busy working to notice anything. The same will go for the photographer, videographer, master of ceremonies. We were all rushed off our feet. You remember seeing Sophie in a penguin costume, don't you? We didn't have a minute to spare at that wedding. Even I had to do a costume change.'

Clare interrupted Saffie's nervous outburst. 'We're so sorry to hear your news, Eloise. We'll cancel your wedding booking and contact the suppliers. Unfortunately, we won't be able to refund your deposit, it's less than six weeks to what would have been your big day. There's a clause in our Terms & Conditions to that effect.'

Eloise sighed. 'Whatever. My father paid the deposit; he won't need money where he's going. It's just a shame the apartment didn't go through before he was arrested. It's back on the market.'

Sophie helped Eloise to her feet. 'I'll take you to

your car. Are you sure you're OK to drive? If there's anything we can do for you during this unfortunate time, please don't hesitate to let us know.'

*

Clare and Sophie wheeled their chairs along the sparkling porcelain floor to sit opposite Saffie. Clare spoke first, 'Well, I didn't see that coming.' She stared at Saffie. 'You were rambling on a bit. I had to cut in.'

Saffie lowered her eyes. Although she didn't trust Ben, she wouldn't divulge his secret. At least what he'd told her added up. 'I was shocked. Arthur Bloomfield is an old acquaintance of my father's. I was struggling to know what to say.'

Sophie leant back in her chair. 'Now it's sinking in; I'm quite relieved. Managing that wedding would have been a nightmare. Eloise was very reluctant to use us, and she despised Saffie so much she nearly pushed her into the pool.'

Saffie leant forward on her desk. 'What?!'

Clare backed Sophie up. 'It was at the promotional event. I saw her push you, but Ben caught you, so everything worked out well in the end. I didn't want to make a big thing of it.'

Saffie gulped. It served Eloise right that her father was no longer buying her a penthouse apartment in the

West End. Her mind turned back to the promotional event, and she shivered – Ben had told the truth that time too.

Clare waved an arm in the air to attract Saffie's attention. 'What are you thinking about? You're in a world of your own. I've offered to make a round of coffees. Would you like your usual?'

Saffie rubbed her forehead. 'Yes, please. I was wondering what we should focus on now that we don't have the wedding in November.'

Clare headed for the door. 'Let me tell you. We need to get on top of last week's emails first and foremost. That will take a team effort – they need to be cleared down today, or we'll get in a terrible mess. Our next priority is a Christmas Wedding in Scotland. Once we've got that booked in, we should contact three couples with smaller requirements between now and December. There's going to be no time to waste.'

Clare closed the door, and Saffie and Sophie looked at one another. Sophie did a little clap. 'This is so exciting. Trust Clare to keep on top of things while we . . .' Sophie stared at Saffie with guilt written all over her face.

Saffie blushed. 'While we had fun with the Brooker brothers. Well, I don't know about you, but I'm focused on the business from now on. We can't lean on Clare like we did last week.'

Sophie saluted. 'I'm on the case. I'll clear down at least ten emails before she gets back with the coffees.'

Saffie felt a warm sense of pride. She hoped her father would be happy with her. Her parents were coming home tomorrow from the Far East – she couldn't wait to update them on her new business.

14

INVESTOR UPDATE

Vivienne Hamilton-Smythe hugged her daughter. 'Oh, Saffronella, I've missed you so much. How's your wedding business going? I can't believe your father agreed to invest in it to such an extent. It's a worry that Sophie and Clare have given up their jobs to work with you. I know you three have always been close but going into business together is such a risk.'

Saffie smiled. 'Stop frowning, Mummy, or you'll need Botox. I'm delighted to report that my business is booming, even with the cancellation of Eloise Bloomfield's wedding.'

Digby Hamilton-Smythe walked into the room. 'That's what I like to hear; I knew it was a sound investment. I have every faith in my favourite daughter.'

Saffie laughed. 'I'm your only daughter.'

Digby walked over to hug her. 'Now tell me what old Arthur Bloomfield's been up to.'

Saffie sat on the sofa next to her father. 'Well, you'll have read about the drugs gang but, before that happened, I had a feeling the Bloomfields didn't like us. The Coolridges aren't fans of ours either. Did you trip Jamie's father up before the 100 metres at Eton?'

Digby burst out laughing. 'I was already in the blocks – he tripped over his shoelace! Unfortunately, successful people aren't always popular. I've come to learn there are a few green-eyed monsters out there.'

Saffie reached out to hold her father's hand. 'Doesn't that worry you?'

Digby shook his head. 'Definitely not. Now, come along, tell me all about your new business. I've seen the reviews on your website.'

Saffie jumped up and returned with a copy of the Management Summary that Clare had produced. 'Have a read of this. We've been working flat out since we started in June. We've managed two weddings already in London and Majorca. Our promotional event was a huge success, and we have a whole raft of suppliers wanting to work with us.'

Digby raised his eyebrows. 'I'm sure suppliers want to work with you, but what about clients? How many weddings have you got on your order book?'

Saffie suddenly felt nervous. 'One at Christmas in Scotland, four in London next year, and two the following year. And that's just at the moment – we have enquiries coming through all the time. Then there are smaller requirements we are happy to take on. Oh, and I've been meaning to ask if we can use our gardens for small wedding celebrations if there's a demand?'

Digby studied the report, and Vivienne glanced at Saffie before speaking, 'Saffronella's doing so well, isn't she? I never expected her business to take off so quickly. People plan their weddings years in advance. I thought it would be a slow burner, but I was wrong. Our daughter must be doing something right.'

Digby bit his tongue before looking up at Saffie, whose shoulders had slumped. 'It's a promising start. Long may it continue.'

Vivienne clapped her hands. 'We're so proud of you, darling. Of course, you can use our gardens for a party or two. We'll fully support that.'

Digby closed the Management Summary and handed it back to his daughter. 'Good work. You know where I am if you hit any hurdles.'

Saffie couldn't help feeling like her father had just read her school report. 'Thank you. I'll let you know if there are any problems. How long are you home for this time?'

Digby stood up and checked his watch. 'Four days. You must excuse me; I have a teleconference in five minutes. I'm sure you and your mother have a lot to catch up on.'

*

Over dinner that evening, Vivienne questioned her husband: 'Why didn't you give more encouragement to Saffronella earlier? Are the figures looking bad?'

Digby placed his knife and fork on the table and wiped his mouth on a serviette. 'The figures are looking good. I knew Clare would be an asset to Saffronella's team; she won't let the ship sink.'

'Why are you so down in the mouth about it then?'

'I don't want our daughter to take her eye off the ball.'

'Oh, she won't. I've never seen her so excited about anything. I think you're being a sourpuss because she's not interested in joining the family firm. I told you Real Estate wouldn't suit her.'

Digby's eyes twinkled as he'd picked up his cutlery. He may not have a daughter who was interested in the business, but he'd found someone who was. A weight had lifted from his shoulders now he'd recruited a protégé. He'd mention that to his wife and daughter at some point. Digby let out a little chuckle.

'What are you laughing at?'

'You're right, it was my preference for Saffronella to take over from me, but I've moved on from that now. I think our daughter has my ambitious streak, though; the crafty girl is already offering our gardens for hire on her website. I've been keeping an eye on her; there are no flies on me.'

It was now Vivienne's turn to giggle. 'You don't mind, do you? We're hardly ever here.'

'Of course I don't mind. The wedding Saffronella's managing at Christmas will scupper our plans, though. There's no point in us coming home to London if she's not here.'

Vivienne frowned before smiling. 'You have a point there. Why don't we find out where the wedding is and book somewhere close by? We can surprise her. Scotland is beautiful in winter.'

Digby gave a thumbs up to his wife as he chewed on his steak. Now that was an excellent idea. He could imagine staying in a castle with snow-covered grounds overlooking a frozen loch. Digby pierced a chip with his fork before devouring it. He pictured the look of surprise on his daughter's face. Christmas this year was going to be fun!

15

WEDDING CELEBRATION

Clare shivered in her skeleton outfit. Who on earth would want to celebrate their wedding at Halloween? It had taken days to decorate the garden. Even the summer house had been adorned with orange and white twinkling lights as a base for the guests to flock to when they gave up on the stupid scavenger hunt the bride and groom had requested.

Sophie appeared as an angel. Clare raised her eyebrows. 'Why on earth are you wearing that?'

'I thought I'd lighten things up a bit; Halloween is always so spooky. I was only told to turn up in fancy dress.'

Saffie walked into the office in her short white

skater dress. She'd adapted her "uniform" by wearing a pair of orange and black striped woolly tights, black cloak and orange felt hat embroidered with a smiley pumpkin face. 'Isn't this just the weirdest way to celebrate a wedding? Thank goodness the garden is walled off. We wouldn't want to lose any guests. That reminds me, Sophie, you're in charge of the CCTV until everyone is here. At that point, you need to close the electric gates.'

The bride and groom arrived dressed as Dracula and Morticia Addams. Clare whispered to Sophie. 'That's not a good start. Wasn't Morticia married to Gomez? She's cheating on him already with Dracula.'

Sophie giggled. 'Don't make me laugh; I've already split one seam of this angel costume. I knew I should have come as a werewolf!'

When all the guests had arrived, Saffie clinked a crystal glass with a knife. The very act of doing so took her back to Majorca. She sighed. Had she been wrong to avoid Ben since they returned? She frowned; come to think of it, he hadn't tried to get in touch with her either. Clare gave Saffie a nudge, and she cleared her head before speaking, 'As you all know, Debbie and Callum were officially married this morning. As massive fans of horror movies, they wanted to celebrate their union with you all tonight on the most frightening night of the year – Halloween. Please help yourselves to glasses of champagne before following the trail my colleagues – the skeleton and angel – have prepared for you. The first guest back will win Spooky, the cuddly black cat.' Clare waved a large stuffed toy in the air, and Sophie sounded a starting horn.

With the happy couple and their guests roaming the gardens for the next hour or so, the team had time to spare. Saffie filed her nails. 'Did the photographer turn up? I didn't see her at the start of the scavenger hunt.'

Sophie was eating a gingerbread witch and staining her teeth black in the process. Clare pulled her face at the sight before answering Saffie, 'Yes, the photographer's here. She's dressed as a ghost.'

Saffie swivelled round in her chair. 'Good. I can see the catering team setting up by the pool. At least the happy couple requested hot food for their guests after an hour of roaming around in the dark. It was a good idea of yours, Clare, to switch the floodlights on in that area. The pumpkin lanterns are fine for the rest of the garden but too dim where there's water about.'

Sophie pulled a worried face. 'There's water in the lake too.'

Saffie shrugged. 'The trail you two have designed doesn't go near the lake; besides all the footpaths are lit up. If there are any stragglers, they just need to get onto a path to find their way back here. How difficult is that?'

Sophie checked her phone and giggled. Clare raised an eyebrow. 'What are you laughing at?'

'Oh, just a photo that Dean sent me.'

Saffie's ears pricked up. 'Are you still in touch with him?'

Sophie laughed. 'Of course I'm still in touch with him; he's one of our suppliers. I've not heard from Ben, but I'm sure that's because he's in touch with you. Why go to one of the staff when you can get to the boss?'

Saffie lowered her eyes. 'Well, you're wrong. I haven't heard from Ben since we left Majorca.' She stood up. 'I'm going to check on the smoke machine. Where did you leave it again?'

Sophie pointed past the swimming pool. 'It's four trees from the end of the hunt. I was going to switch it on in ten minutes.'

Saffie stood up. 'I'll do it. I need some fresh air.'

When Saffie had left the office, Clare spoke to Sophie, 'It sounds like Ben's done a runner again. You could always ask Dean where his brother is. That way, we'll find out whether the elusive Ben Brooker's been "abducted" again.'

Sophie raised a thumb in the air before sending a message. Her phone soon buzzed with a response from Dean. 'Ben's in touch with Dean; he's just busy with work.'

Clare raised an eyebrow and was about to speak before she jumped up to look out of the window. 'What on earth?!'

Sophie let out a scream. 'Oh, no, no, no, no, no!! Saffie didn't turn the machine around the right way!' Sophie ran out of the summer house and headed towards the swimming pool, but she couldn't see through the smoke. 'Saffieeee! Can you hear me? You need to turn the smoke machine off and stop everyone heading for the pool.'

Saffie stood next to the machine. A ghost with a camera appeared next to her; it bent down and flicked the "off" switch. Saffie's heart was pounding. 'What did I do wrong?'

The ghost raised its arms in the air. 'The machine was facing the wrong way.'

Saffie stood still – she was shocked and dumbfounded. There could have been a very nasty accident. Clare needed to check the company's insurance covered such events. As it was, the smoke needed to clear before the wedding party could reach their food. Saffie just hoped she could spot the winner of Spooky the cat.

Five minutes later, there was a winner who Saffie

clung onto until the smoke dispersed. Ten minutes later, Debbie and Callum walked arm in arm towards Saffie. The sight of Morticia and Dracula approaching was a huge relief. 'Well done, you two! You made it back safely! Please make your way to the pool area where hot food is about to be served.'

Dracula threw his arm around Saffie. 'This has been better than we imagined. We will be recommending you to our friends.'

Saffie managed a weak smile. 'That's very kind of you. Please leave a review on our website.'

The smoke had lifted, giving Sophie and Clare a clear view of Frankenstein walking around with a cuddly black cat under his arm. They both giggled before giving each other high fives. Clare spoke first, 'Thank goodness this is nearly over. We can focus on Christmas in Scotland from tomorrow.'

Sophie grinned. 'I can't wait to see Dean again. It's great he can do the videography.'

Clare shuddered. At least this time, there would only be one Brooker brother there. Surely Saffie would pull her weight at such a high profile wedding of a famous couple that would hit the press.

16

CHRISTMAS IN SCOTLAND

Summer and Nathaniel were Australian soap stars who had chosen to marry in Scotland. Saffie shivered as she looked out of the castle window. Surely a sunny winter wedding in Australia would be preferable to a cold, bleak one in Scotland? It had been snowing since the beginning of December, and now – with two days to go – there were flight cancellations, road closures and reluctant wedding suppliers who would prefer to spend Christmas with their family and friends.

Sophie twirled around in excitement. 'Dean's nearly here. He said the journey was horrendous, but he can't wait to see me. This is going to be our best wedding yet!'

Saffie felt a pang of guilt; her parents would be in

Barbados by now. They had understood that she couldn't be home for Christmas, but she knew they were upset. She decided to message them:

> *Hi Mummy and Daddy, we made it safely to Scotland. The castle is amazing. I can't help but envy you both, though, it's sooooo cold here, my feet are freezing. Still, we couldn't turn down a wedding like this. Make sure you look out for the photographs in the UK and Australian press. I've got a busy time ahead but will call you on Christmas Day. Love you lots, Saffronella xxx*

*

Digby Hamilton-Smythe lifted his feet onto a footstool and relaxed as the heat of a roaring fire warmed his toes. He called out to his wife, 'That was a jolly bracing walk through the snow. Old Alistair's being a good sport letting us use this cottage in the grounds of his castle. At least I still have some friends from Eton.'

Vivienne entered the room. 'Have you seen the message from Saffronella? She'll be so shocked when she sees us! Your friend seems quite taken by our daughter and her team. He says they're very polite and professional.'

Digby sighed; he was sad that Saffronella didn't want to join the family business. Still, his new protégé was performing well. It was just a matter of time until he divulged the news to his wife and daughter that, when he retired, he intended the business to remain in the family.

*

Back at the castle, Dean shook the snow off his overcoat while Ben wheeled their cases through the great hallway. Sophie stopped in her tracks at the sight of them. 'I didn't know Ben was coming.'

Dean stepped forward to hug her. 'It's Christmas! I couldn't let my brother be alone over the holidays. He'll be bunking down with me. I've got a twin room, so there's plenty of space.'

*

Clare sat in the room designated as an office for their stay. It overlooked the front gardens and winding driveway. Summer and Nathaniel were due to arrive in the next half hour. How lovely of them to hold their wedding in Scotland to cater for Summer's ageing grandmother. Clare scanned her emails. It seemed like the world's press would be present on Christmas Day. The happy couple were easy-going and keen to "share their love". That made Clare's job a lot harder. She'd need to organise barriers outside and hot drinks and perhaps some warm mince pies to alleviate the chance of any frozen members of the paparazzi.

The door to the "office" opened. 'I'm not

disturbing you, am I?'

Clare sat up straight at the sight of the laird. 'Not at all, Sir.'

The laird smiled. 'Call me Alistair. Now, is there anything my wife and I can do to help you?'

Clare shook her head. 'That's very kind of you, but we have everything in control – it's our job. We hope we don't cause you any disturbance. May I ask where you and your family will be staying over Christmas, now that you've hired out your home?'

Alistair walked to a window and pointed down the drive. 'In one of the cottages. It'll make a nice change for us.' The laird's eyes teared up. 'It will be the first Christmas we're without our children. Lizzie's in Aspen and Cameron's in Dubai.'

Clare didn't know what to say; she was saved by the sound of tyres on the gravel outside. 'That'll be the bride and groom. We should go and greet them. They'll be so impressed to meet you.'

*

Saffie stared at Sophie. 'What do you mean "Ben's here"?'

'Dean brought him along for Christmas.'

'Can't he spend it with his parents?'

Sophie glared at Saffie. 'The boys were brought up by their father, who passed away earlier this year. Their mother died when they were very young. I thought you'd know that from the amount of time you spent with Ben in Majorca. Didn't you ask anything about him?'

Saffie blushed; come to think of it, she'd mainly talked about her. Ben knew her life story, and she didn't know much about him at all except that he had a brother, a yacht, and he'd been instrumental in getting two men arrested – but that was, of course, a secret.

*

Digby threw another log on the fire, and Vivienne sat on the edge of her chair. 'When can we meet up with Saffronella?'

Digby's eyes twinkled. 'We'll be seeing her tonight. I've arranged a small private party at the pub over the road. Alistair and Isla have invited Saffronella, Clare, Sophie, the videographer, and his brother. Apparently, they're all very close. They worked together on that wedding in Majorca.'

Vivienne clapped her hands. 'How very exciting! It sounds like more fun than working in Real Estate. I can see how appealing it would be to Saffronella. I wonder if the videographer and his brother are handsome?'

Digby shrugged. 'I wouldn't know. You can make that judgement later.'

*

After an initial meeting with the bride and groom and a tour of the castle, Saffie checked her watch. She needed to wrap things up as the laird was taking them all to the pub at six o'clock, and she wanted to shower and change first.

'We have a full schedule for tomorrow. The ceremony and function rooms will be set up and decorated in your lavender and peach colour scheme. We have a hair and make-up trial scheduled for Summer in the morning, the celebrant will be here in the afternoon to have a run-through with you both, and a team of florists will be here throughout the day.'

Summer hugged Saffie. 'Thank you so much. We couldn't have done this without you.'

Saffie smiled. 'There's just one more thing; all your meals will be served in the dining room from tonight until the morning after your wedding. We have advised the chef of the number of guests expected at each one. We are so excited to be working with you on the arrangements for your special day.'

Nathaniel held out his hand to shake Saffie's. 'It's

all sounding great. Any chance you've got Foster's on tap?'

Saffie nodded. 'Of course.' She waved as Summer and Nathaniel headed off to their room and said a silent prayer of thanks that Clare had organised the delivery of Australian lager for the event. Now, what should she wear tonight? She'd have brought something special if she'd known Ben would be here.

17

FAMILY NIGHT OUT

Saffie pulled her long coat around her on the walk down the castle drive to the pub. How on earth Sophie had ignored her request to take the silver dress to the charity shop – and had thought of bringing it to Scotland – was beyond belief. Saffie could only imagine that Sophie had planned to wear it herself for a romantic evening with Dean. Well, bad luck with that! At least Sophie had a conscience and had left it on Saffie's bed for *her* to wear.

Alistair held the pub door open, and the girls walked through. Ben and Dean had got there earlier. Saffie took off her coat and handed it to Sophie as she looked around the pub. Before she knew it she was accosted by her mother. 'Saffronella! Surprise, surprise. We couldn't bear to spend Christmas without you!'

Saffie was aghast. Weren't her parents in Barbados?

Digby poked his daughter on the shoulder, and she turned around. 'You didn't think your mother would let you desert us at Christmas, did you?'

Saffie's mouth fell open as she hugged her father before her mother complained about her attire. 'Don't you think that dress is a bit much for a quaint old place like this? Would you like to borrow my cardigan?'

Saffie huffed as her eyes searched for Ben. 'Why don't you two go and sit down? I'll be over shortly.'

Ben was at the bar, and Saffie joined him. He handed her a glass of wine before whispering, 'The dress looks great.'

Vivienne leant forward in her seat for a better look. She nudged Digby. 'He's rather nice. There's definite chemistry between Dean and our daughter.'

Digby lowered his eyes. 'His name's Benjamin.'

Vivienne tutted. 'Silly me to get the brothers mixed up – they're both very handsome. Saffronella should formally introduce us. I'll ask her to bring Benjamin over.'

Saffie and Ben sat down opposite her parents, and Vivienne beamed across at them. 'Well then, I'll let you do the introductions, Saffronella. How did you meet this nice young man?'

Saffie was horrified. How could her mother be so embarrassing? What was she supposed to say? She took a gulp of wine and forced a smile before responding, 'This is Benjamin Brooker. He's a videographer we've worked with on a couple of occasions.'

Vivienne noticed Ben's blushes. She didn't care what Saffronella said; there was definitely something between the two of them. 'How lovely.'

Ben held out his hand to shake Vivienne's and Digby's. 'I'm very pleased to meet you, Mr and Mrs Hamilton-Smythe.'

Vivienne's eyes twinkled. 'There's no need to be so formal. Please call us Vivienne and Digby.'

Saffie glanced around the room before standing up. 'Please excuse me. I need to discuss some wedding arrangements with Clare.'

Vivienne sighed. 'Can't you have a night off? All work and no play will make you a dull girl.'

Saffie shook her head. 'We're on duty until after the wedding. It's lovely that you've come to Scotland to see me, and I'll make sure we catch up over Christmas, I promise. But, right now, I have work to do.'

With that, Saffie walked over to the far side of the

bar, leaving a very uncomfortable Ben with her parents. Vivienne felt a coolness from Digby and was relieved when Alistair and Isla asked to join them. That was an ideal opportunity for Ben to make his exit, and he made a beeline for Saffie.

'Thanks for leaving me with your parents.'

Saffie raised her eyes. 'My mother is so embarrassing, I had to make a quick exit, or she'd be planning *our* wedding.'

Ben's eyes sparkled. 'Would that be so bad?'

Saffie blushed. 'Well, it would be pretty difficult when you keep disappearing. I haven't heard from you since Majorca.'

Ben grinned. 'I haven't heard from you either. You must have been thinking of me though, if you're taking that dress everywhere on the off chance I'll turn up.'

Saffie huffed. 'It's not like that. I asked Sophie to take it to a charity shop, and, for some reason, she brought it here instead. I can only guess she was planning to wear it herself.'

Ben took hold of Saffie's hand. 'Well, I'm not difficult to get hold of over the next few days.'

Alistair's wife, Isla, was the most welcoming person you could wish to meet. She'd already invited Vivienne and Digby for Christmas lunch. 'I will not take "no" for an answer. Your daughter and her team can pop in and out of our temporary home all day, although I know they'll be busy with the wedding at the castle.'

Vivienne was quick to spot an opportunity. 'That's very kind of you, Isla; we'll be delighted to accept your invitation. Of course, it's not just Saffronella and her team who are away from home on Christmas Day; there are those two nice young men too. They're all very close, and I'm sure they'll be delighted to escape from the wedding to spend time in your cosy cottage.'

Digby was well aware that Saffronella was choosing to spend time with Ben down the other end of the bar. Although she was out of sight, he could hear her laughter. When she checked on her parents, he had a quiet word with her. 'Benjamin Brooker is a videographer; he's in no way marriage material for a daughter of mine. I'll be polite to him over Christmas, but he doesn't have my approval going forward.'

Vivienne slapped a hand to her mouth, and Saffie's eyes glistened. She held her shoulders back. 'Don't be so silly, Daddy. I've already told you; Benjamin Brooker is a supplier of ours. I have no romantic interest in him whatsoever. I just came to let you know I'll be heading back to the castle shortly. There'll be no late nights for me this week. I'll let Clare and Sophie know, and I'll no doubt see you both at some stage tomorrow.'

Saffie kissed her parents and went to find her friends. On her way past Ben, she stopped to whisper in his ear, 'I'm in Room 12. I'll leave it unlocked.'

18

CHRISTMAS EVE

Saffie hung the silver dress in her closet. She decided it was a "lucky" dress now – it had broken the ice between her and Ben. She sighed when she thought back to her father's words in the pub. Unfortunately, he didn't approve of Ben, but that didn't matter. There was every chance Ben would do another disappearing act after Christmas. Saffie just had to make the most of him while he was around.

*

Vivienne continued to be annoyed with Digby. 'You still haven't given me a good reason why you've taken offence to Benjamin. I talked to Sophie last night, and she says he owns a yacht. Being a videographer may only be a hobby for him. I can tell he's suited to our daughter – you can't interfere with chemistry.'

Digby shrugged his shoulders. 'I have someone in mind for Saffronella. I haven't mentioned this before, but I've hired a protégé.'

'A protégé?'

'Yes. A person who will take over from me when I retire. My aim is that he'll also marry our daughter and, that way, the business will stay in our family.'

Vivienne's knees buckled, and she flopped back onto a sofa. 'I've never heard of anything so ridiculous. You know what Saffronella's like – she won't be pushed into a corner. I can't believe you're in support of arranged marriages. I'm lost for words.'

Digby threw a log onto the fire. 'It's all about thinking out of the box.'

Vivienne's heart was pounding; she lifted her legs onto the sofa to lie down. 'Don't give me that corporate rubbish. It's our daughter's happiness we're talking about here.'

Digby walked over and patted his wife's shoulder. 'There, there. Don't you worry – I believe in happy endings too. I'll pop into the kitchen and make you a cup of tea.'

Vivienne grabbed her husband's hand. 'What does your protégé look like? Does he have nice teeth? She'll insist on nice teeth.'

Digby smiled. 'They look fine to me.'

'What colour eyes?'

'Green.'

'Hair colour?'

'Black.'

Vivienne sat up. 'I'm beginning to feel better already. If we manage to get Saffronella settled down *and* keep the business in the family, we'll have everything we've ever wished for.'

*

The press had started to gather outside the castle. Photographs of the bride and groom on the lead up to their big day were in demand. Clare needn't have worried about providing refreshments; Isla was on the case. She had time on her hands with a chef and catering staff booked for today and tomorrow to assist in their cottage. Isla put on her thermals and walked towards the castle armed with mince pies and sausage rolls.

Nathaniel was also at a loss. Summer was having a hair and make-up trial, and he decided to go for a brisk walk. He strode through the castle doors to a burst of camera flashes. Isla waved to him, but he chose to ignore her. That was the last thing he needed, fans turning up before the wedding. Nathaniel shivered, not just because of the cold but because of the concern that one particular fan may turn up.

The cameras flashed again as the castle doors opened to the sight of Ben and Dean. Ben waved an arm in the air. 'Sorry guys, we're not famous or guests at the wedding. We're in the photography business like you. It's a cold day for it today. Let's hope you get some good shots.'

One of the photographers called the brothers over. 'Hey guys, I'm having some issues with my gear. Any chance you could take a look?' Once they were next to him, he brought up an image on his screen and spoke softly. 'Have you seen this woman inside the castle? I captured her lurking in the bushes this morning.'

The men shook their heads. Ben raised his eyebrows. 'Maybe we should flag it up to security?'

The photographer was aghast. 'I thought you two could be trusted, fellow photographers and the like. I'm in for a big pay-out when I expose her.'

Dean's eagle eyes were drawn to the castle. 'Quick. Third window from the right, ground floor.'

The photographer clicked away. 'Thanks, mate! That's a great Christmas bonus for me.'

*

By early evening, the castle was decorated to perfection. Flowers adorned an arch around the entrance doors, and the ceremony and function rooms were filled with roses and lilies. Christmas trees embellished with lavender and peach baubles stood tall in each room, creating a seasonal scent of pine.

Saffie and her team felt their chests bursting with pride; they had pulled out all the stops for this wedding. It was going to be their best one yet. Images of this would look amazing on their website. They left the happy couple to spend a quiet moment on their own in the ceremony room while they made a final check of the place names in the function room.

Clare put a finger to her lips. 'Shush. Was that a sob?'

Sophie gasped. 'It was a scream.'

Saffie ran into the corridor then poked her head back into the room. 'They're arguing. What should we do?'

Clare sat on a banqueting chair. 'Come back in here. It'll just be a lover's tiff. Stop being nosy, close the door and give them time to work their way through it.' Saffie and Sophie sat down too.

The shouting grew louder. Saffie cringed. 'I hope they don't break anything.' She jumped up. 'That was a definite door slam. We should check what's going on.'

The girls ventured into the corridor to find Summer in a flood of tears. 'It's off! The wedding's off. He's been cheating on me, and it's all over social media.'

19

CHRISTMAS MORNING

The press outside the castle had dispersed as soon as they'd captured shots of Summer and Nathaniel departing separately last night. Alistair and Isla now had their home back to themselves and the luxury of seven guests to join them for Christmas lunch. It had been too late for Clare, Sophie, and the Brooker brothers to make alternative arrangements.

Vivienne was delighted; she could now spend more time with her daughter. She felt a bit uncomfortable about Benjamin being there but knew her husband had a plan in place that would benefit Saffronella more.

Ben glanced at his brother. 'We chose the wrong career. We could have made a fortune as members of the paparazzi. With your detective work and my photography skills, we'd have been a great team.'

Dean chuckled. 'That guy was certainly onto something. Can you believe he held onto photographic evidence for a whole two weeks until he had an amazing collection that someone's paid a fortune for?'

Ben sighed. 'I feel sorry for the bride.'

Dean shrugged. 'It would have been much worse for her if that fan had turned up today at the part where they ask: *If any person here present knows of any reason why the happy couple should not be married* – or words to that effect. That's what she was planning to do – she'd flown here from Australia.'

Ben rubbed his chin. 'I read about that too. What a loser, having an affair with a fan when he had such a stunning fiancée.'

Dean raised his eyebrows. 'She's nothing like Saffie. Don't tell me your head would turn if you had the chance?'

It was Ben's turn to shrug. 'There's nothing serious between us. Besides, I have a distinct feeling her father disapproves of me.'

Dean finished his coffee before slapping his brother on the back. 'I expect you're still too busy for a relationship. Are you off to far-flung places again in the New Year?'

Ben's eyes twinkled. 'I certainly am.'

*

Isla dragged her overnight bag along the gravel driveway to the castle. The flowers outside were beautiful. She took the time to sniff the roses before leaving her case in the hallway and heading off to the rooms that were decorated for the ceremony and wedding breakfast.

Isla caught her breath; she had never seen the castle looking so spectacular. She made a decision there and then and headed for the kitchen.

With the catering team hired for the wedding relieved from their duties, the small group of staff previously helping in the cottage stood around scratching their heads.

Isla smiled. 'I know this is different from what we had planned. First, it was lunch in the cottage, and then we moved it to the dining room here, but I've just been in the room that's set up for the wedding breakfast, and it smells so lovely. It would be a shame not to use such a pretty setting. I notice the round tables are laid for ten people. As there will be nine of us for lunch, we'll use one of those.'

*

Saffie knocked on the door of her parents' cottage. Her

mother opened it. 'Happy Christmas, darling! Would you like to open your presents now or later?'

Saffie was in shock. The celebrity wedding she was organising had crashed, her parents had turned up, Ben was available – nothing was going to plan. 'Oh, Mummy, I haven't brought your presents to Scotland. I left them in London for when we're due to meet up next.'

Vivienne smiled. 'Of course, you did. We'll be back in London soon enough. Why don't you open your presents now, it'll distract your father. He's been making business calls on Christmas Day – something we never allow him to do at home.'

Digby ended a call when Saffie entered the room. 'Happy Christmas, Saffronella! I've arranged for a drop of Bucks Fizz and your mother's making bacon sandwiches. It's good to use the kitchen while we're here. Isla's been great with providing provisions.'

Saffie hugged her father. 'I've missed you both. I can't believe you're here.'

Digby held an arm around his daughter. 'There's been a lot of change for you this year. It's good to have a safe island to cling to.'

Vivienne walked in with a tray of Bucks Fizz. 'I know I've put on weight, but there's no need to call me an island!'

Saffie laughed as she raised her glass. 'I love you both so much. Happy Christmas!'

*

Sophie was stunned. A large bouquet of red roses had arrived for Clare. Her friend read the card before putting it in her bag. 'Well, who are they from?'

Clare waved a hand in the air. 'Just an acquaintance.'

Sophie's phone buzzed with a message from Dean:

Meet me in the ceremony room in ten minutes.

Her heart leapt. 'I'm just popping downstairs for a bit; I need to check on things.'

Dean stood in his pyjama bottoms, holding a bunch of peach roses. 'Happy Christmas, Sophie!'

Sophie covered her eyes with her hands and looked through her fingers. 'You shouldn't be walking around the castle like that, let alone stealing wedding flowers.'

Dean chuckled as he threw his arms around her. 'Here, take the roses. It's the best I could do at short notice. I'll take you out for a meal when we're both in London.'

*

Ben shook the snow off the boots he'd borrowed from Alistair. He'd been for a long winter's walk to clear his head – it hadn't worked. What was he going to do about Saffronella? He wanted her, but he couldn't have her. He had to focus on the next stage of his life, and Saffronella was off limits.

One thing was for sure – next year would be the making of him. Ben held his shoulders back and let all thoughts of Saffronella drift to the back of his mind. There was a time and place for everything; this was the time for him to grab the opportunity that faced him with both hands.

20

CHRISTMAS AFTERNOON

Alistair raised his glass. 'To our new friends, Happy Christmas, and good health to you all!'

Digby raised his glass too. 'Here's to you and Isla for welcoming us into your home.'

Glasses clinked before serviettes were placed on laps at the sight of the first course of smoked salmon being wheeled into the room. Vivienne turned to Isla. 'It must be wonderful living in a castle.'

Isla smiled. 'Yes, it is. It's a lot of work, though, and it costs a fortune to maintain. We manage with the minimum of staff.'

Saffie leant forward. 'Well, we'd certainly like to use your home for future weddings. We know where everything is now, and it would be lovely to see you and Alistair again. Would you agree for us to promote your castle as a wedding venue on our website?'

Isla clapped her hands. 'Please do!'

Sophie nudged Clare. 'Go on, tell me, who sent the flowers?'

Clare averted her eyes. 'They're from my family.'

Sophie smirked – her friend was being devious. She could tell when Clare was lying. Now, why would she want to keep her admirer secret? When did Clare have time for an admirer anyway? She worked harder at the business than Saffie and Sophie put together. Clare only took time off on Wednesday evenings when she went to the gym.

Dean grabbed Sophie's knee under the table. 'Do you like the flowers?'

Sophie whispered in his ear, 'I love them. You're so thoughtful.'

Digby sat next to Ben, and Saffie wished Isla had provided place names rather than it turn into a free for all when everyone sat down. Her father looked uncomfortable. The main course had arrived, and he was tucking into roast turkey with all the trimmings. He wasn't making an effort to speak to Ben at all. Saffie decided to change that. She called across the table,

'Ben, why don't you tell my father about your trip to the South of France? We went there all the time when I was younger.'

Ben gulped, and Dean tried to help him out. There was definite friction between his brother and Saffie's father. 'I have a better idea. Why don't you tell us where you're off to in the New Year? I'd be keen to know how you're chosen to go to all these far-flung places. I've only got bookings in the UK in my diary for next year. Come to think of it, I only made it to Majorca as your substitute.'

Ben smiled. 'It's all about networking. Now let's change the subject of business. I'd like to hear if Isla and Alistair have monsters in their loch.'

Digby placed his knife and fork down. 'A loch! I wanted to see a loch. Where is it?'

Alistair laughed. 'I'm surprised you missed it on your walk. I'll take you there after lunch. And, in answer to Ben's question, yes, we do have a few monsters, fairies, and the like.'

Isla nodded. 'We sure do. You have to be in the right frame of mind to see them, though.'

Digby chuckled as he picked up his glass of Chardonnay. 'I'll be of the right mindset before we get there! It's always good to get the most out of an experience.'

Saffie sighed. So, Ben was off again in the New Year – she wasn't surprised. It was best to keep Benjamin Brooker at arm's length; men like him couldn't be tied down. She could feel him staring at her across the table, so she raised her head to stare back. Why did he have to be so ruggedly handsome? His brown hair was never tidy, yet it framed his face to perfection – and those eyes – well, they reminded her of a blue sky on a perfect summer's day.

Clare pulled Saffie's serviette off her lap. 'Come along, daydreamer. You've got the choice of a brisk cold walk to the loch or a lesson in Gin Rummy with Isla and your mother.'

Saffie pushed her chair back, and Ben caught hold of her arm. He winked at Clare. 'Saffronella and I have our own plans.'

When the couple were alone, Ben took hold of her hands. 'What were you planning to wear today? No – let me guess. It was supposed to be a wedding day, so you'd be wearing your short white skater dress. Am I correct?'

Saffie tilted her head to one side. 'Nearly. This was going to be a winter wedding, so I added an item to my uniform.'

Ben raised an eyebrow. 'A tiara?'

Saffie giggled. 'Wrong! A white fur bolero.'

Ben nodded his approval. 'I can't wait to see it. Go and get changed and meet me in the ceremony room in fifteen minutes.'

Saffie's heart pounded. That man was far too exciting to be on the loose. Women must be dropping at his feet everywhere. She didn't like the thought of that, so she focused on the present. Ben was hers – if just for today – and she intended to make the most of it.

Twelve minutes later, Saffie bounded into the ceremony room to be met by the sight of Ben with his camera. His face lit up at the sight of her. 'Wow! You look amazing. You don't mind if I take a few shots, do you? It's a shame to waste all the effort your team has put into this non-event.'

Saffie's heart sank. All Ben wanted was a free model. The images would no doubt be displayed all over his website. Ben opened a bottle of champagne and poured two glasses. As he handed one to Saffie, he noticed a head bobbing up and down through a window. The couple were shortly joined by Dean. 'Am I pleased to see you two! It's freezing out there, and the only other option is Gin Rummy with Isla and Vivienne. I'd much prefer to be in here with you. Do you have another glass?' Dean noticed a tray of empty glasses and went over to pick one up. 'What are you doing in here anyway? Why's Saffie in her uniform?'

Ben blushed. 'I thought Saffronella would look good in some shots with the amazing background in this room. The Christmas tree, in particular, looks spectacular.'

Dean's creative mind kicked in. 'Brilliant idea, bro. Saffie looks like a trendy bride in that dress. You could be a cool groom in those dove grey trousers and white shirt. Take off that cashmere sweater and go and stand next to her. I'll take the photos. If Saffie approves, you can use them on your website – it needs updating.'

*

Over an hour later, Ben let out a sigh of relief. Dean had received a call from Sophie, who was back from the loch. Saffie and Ben were alone at last. They sat on a window seat and viewed the images Dean had taken. Saffie was impressed. 'Dean's a great photographer. You can put them on your website if you wish.'

Ben shook his head. 'I won't do that. I just wanted one or two images of you to take with me.'

Saffie's heart cracked; she knew he was going away, but this sounded final. 'Where are you going?'

Ben's eyes clouded over. 'I can't say.' He walked

over to where he'd left his camera case and produced a small box. 'This is for you to remember me by.'

Saffie burst into tears at the sight of a silver bracelet with three charms: A camera, a rose, and a church. Ben handed her a handkerchief. 'I didn't want you to be upset. The camera and church symbolise both our businesses and the rose – well, that's to make up for the first present I bought you but wasn't able to give you.'

Saffie sobbed as she remembered the vase of pink roses on her desk. 'Why do you have to go away again? Why can't you stay in London?'

Ben held her in his arms and kissed the top of her head. 'Because you deserve better than me. It's as simple as that.'

21

NEW YEAR, NEW PLANS

Saffie sat in her parents' living room in Kensington and sipped the hot chocolate her mother had made. Vivienne was worried. Her daughter had lost weight since Christmas, and she didn't have weight to lose. She had an idea. 'We should go clothes shopping. What do you think?'

Saffie looked over the rim of her mug. 'I need a new uniform.'

Vivienne was pleased with a breakthrough. 'What a brilliant idea! Why don't you change out of those pyjamas, and we'll take a taxi to Oxford Street. That skimpy white dress isn't suitable for the businesswoman you've become.'

Saffie looked down into the depths of her mug. Whatever her mother said or wanted was acceptable; she couldn't care less. Just dragging herself out of bed was a major challenge – Ben had left Scotland on Christmas Day, and she hadn't heard from him since. She fiddled with the silver bracelet on her wrist, and the tears flowed again.

Vivienne chose not to notice. 'I think a nice grey, knee-length, fitted dress will be much more suitable as a uniform. We should add a jacket too. I know just the shop! Drink up, get changed, and we'll be off!'

Being upbeat and acting like things were normal was taking its toll on Vivienne. If she sat down and thought about the situation, she'd burst into tears too. Saffronella loved Benjamin, who kept disappearing for months on end and was undoubtedly leading a playboy lifestyle on his yacht. Then there was Digby, who was adamant their daughter should marry his protégé. Things couldn't get much worse.

Saffie placed her mug on the coffee table. 'Where's Daddy today?'

'Oh, he's playing golf. Some sort of doubles competition he couldn't miss.'

A light bulb switched on in Vivienne's head. 'Come along; there's lots we need to do this morning. Put on a lovely outfit, and I'll order a taxi. Quick! You need to be ready in half an hour.'

*

Saffie sat in the back of the taxi. 'Where are we going? Oxford Street was two turnings back there on the left.'

Vivienne smiled. 'We should pop into your father's office first. I need to use the ladies' cloakroom.'

Saffie frowned. 'Why? The shops have toilets.'

Vivienne's smile was frozen while she thought of another reason. 'Trust me, Saffronella, your father complains I don't show any interest in his business. Well, I'm showing interest now.'

Saffie laughed. 'By going to the toilet in his office when he's not there?'

Vivienne was running out of excuses. 'OK, you've caught me out. Your father has hired a protégé with green eyes, black hair, and nice teeth. He intends to hand the business over to him. I think you and I should check things out while he's at golf.'

Saffie's eyes widened. 'Sounds like a plan.'

*

The Head Office of *Hamilton-Smythe Real Estate* was in Canary Wharf. Saffie felt more energised than she had in weeks. How could her father hand over the family business to a stranger? Her mother was quite right to undertake some detective work.

Vivienne pointed to a building. 'That's the one over there.'

The women waited outside until employees with identity cards opened the doors then followed them in. A security guard stopped them. 'Show me your passes.'

Vivienne took out her driving licence. 'I'm Vivienne Hamilton-Smythe, and this is my daughter, Saffronella. My husband employs you, and you need to let us in. We're only here for a quick visit.' The security guard wasn't going to risk his job by arguing with an older woman who claimed she was married to the company's owner. He decided to turn a blind eye on this occasion.

Vivienne headed for the lift. 'His office is on the top floor.'

As they walked through the main office, Saffie noticed several employees from business events her father had dragged her along to in the past. They waved and smiled as they tried to hide their shocked expressions. Vivienne was on a mission as she whispered to her daughter, 'Let's find him.'

Saffie searched the sea of heads as they strode towards her father's office. There were a couple with black hair but, surely, her father would have given a more prominent desk to his protégé?

Then they spotted him – he sat outside Digby's office. He had black hair, green eyes, and nice teeth, which sparkled when he smiled. 'It's Mrs Hamilton-Smythe, isn't it? And your daughter, Saffronella. Your husband has shown me photographs. My name's Simon Turrinelli. I'm Digby's Executive Assistant.'

Vivienne smiled as she shook hands with Simon. From first impressions, he wasn't too bad at all. 'You have an unusual name. Are you Italian?'

Simon flashed another perfect smile. 'My father is – my mother is British. Did you have a good time in Scotland over Christmas? Digby said you stayed in a castle with a loch. He was full of stories about it when he got back.'

Vivienne's eyes roamed over Simon's expensive handmade suit, the tidiness of his desk and his tanned skin, which signified he'd been to warmer climes than Scotland during the Christmas break. Digby could be onto a winner here. Vivienne suddenly felt very naughty – she should have left things alone and trusted her husband. He'd be livid if he found out she'd tried to interfere. She had to find a way out of this mess.

Saffie sensed her mother's distress, and she answered on her behalf. 'We had a good time, thank you. Now, we need to let you in on a little secret. We're planning a family meal for my father's birthday next week. Is there any chance you could check his diary and let us know if he's available from late afternoon on Thursday?'

Simon tapped away on his computer. 'I can make sure he has no appointments after three o'clock if that helps?'

Saffie feigned a burst of excitement. 'Oh, goody! Thank you so much. We must be off now. Please don't mention we popped in. We'll no doubt be introduced to you officially one day. Just forget you ever met us.'

Simon tapped his nose with his forefinger. 'Your secret's safe with me.'

Saffie ushered her mother out of the building. When they were outside, they let out sighs of relief. Vivienne was struggling to contain her excitement. 'I rather like him, don't you?'

Saffie shrugged. 'He's pleasant enough. It's a shame I don't have any siblings interested in Real Estate, but that's just the way it goes. Daddy will need to hand the business over to someone eventually, and Simon seems perfect. Let's hope he can keep a secret; we'll be in for a lot of explaining if he splits on us.'

22

TIME TO TAKE STOCK

March had arrived, and *Weddings by Saffronella* was three-quarters into its first year. Clare had been up all night checking the figures ahead of a meeting with Digby. She was well aware he'd only promised to fund the salaries of her and Sophie for the first year. Today would identify whether they both needed to start looking for new jobs.

Digby sat in his daughter's white swivel chair scrutinising the Management Accounts. He was silent. Sophie bit her nails, and Clare struggled to keep her eyes open. Saffie's heart was thumping. She kept her fingers crossed as she stood next to a window in the summer house, pretending to admire the view.

Finally, Digby closed the report and leant forward on the desk. The girls all turned to face him. They were surprised to see him beam from ear to ear. 'Well, I never thought I'd see the day. My daughter has a career and a decent one at that. I know you've put your heart and soul into it, Saffronella. I'm very proud of you. I also applaud Clare's financial control, along with Sophie's zest for obtaining new business.'

Sophie twisted her hands together. 'So, we've still got jobs?'

Digby nodded. 'Very much so. I expect this business to go from strength to strength.'

Saffie walked over to hug her father. 'I'm sorry I didn't want to join the family business, Daddy. I know that was your preferred choice for me.'

Digby hugged his daughter back. 'All I've ever wanted is for you to be happy. With that in mind, I've been training a protégé who will take over from me in due course. I want you and your mother to meet him.'

Saffie blushed. Simon had indeed kept their secret. It would be awkward meeting him in an official capacity, but it needed to be done. She managed to smile. 'That's such a relief. I hated disappointing you. It's a shame you didn't have a son as well as me.'

Digby grinned. His protégé was everything he could have wished for in a son. He was sure Saffronella would like him too.

*

Going to the pub was the last thing Clare needed. She was exhausted, but Saffie and Sophie were in a buoyant mood and insisted on dragging her along. After the first glass of wine, she perked up. 'I don't know why I was so worried. The figures speak for themselves. I guess there was always a chance your father may pull the plug on us and invest his money elsewhere, but, after today, I'm confident he has every faith in us.'

Sophie beamed. 'I'd started looking for other jobs just in case we didn't make it through the first year, but Digby's in no doubt at all we'll sail through to year-end and that the business will take off from next year.'

Clare grinned at Saffie. 'Your new uniform is helping. A sensible dove grey dress to match our trouser suits isn't putting off any brides.'

Sophie chuckled. 'It's not attracting any grooms either. I'm sure we got a couple of weddings booked in because the grooms had the final say on things.'

Saffie thought back to the short white skater dress; she hadn't worn it since Christmas Day. It hung in her wardrobe next to the silver dress. Her initial upset over Ben had turned to annoyance. He was either a weak man or a charmer who had a girl in every port. She couldn't decide which. He indeed visited a few ports as he travelled the world from what she'd heard from Sophie. The silver bracelet felt cheap, and she chose not to wear it anymore. There were more important things to focus on than Benjamin Brooker – her booming business was at the top of the list.

Sophie checked her emails. 'Oh no! We're off to the Lavender Tree Banqueting Rooms in August. Please don't say I'll need to dress up as a penguin again.'

Saffie laughed. 'I wonder if the manager there recommended us. He was very impressed with our services. What was his name?'

Clare lowered her eyes. 'Heinrich.'

Sophie's head spun around to stare at Saffie as an idea sprang to mind. She turned back to face Clare. 'Heinrich has Wednesdays off. I've made a note of that on the venue's supplier contact sheet.' She watched as a redness crept up Clare's neck onto her cheeks. 'You don't go to the gym on Wednesday nights, do you? You've been seeing tall, dark, handsome, bespectacled Heinrich! He's the one who sent you the red roses at Christmas. It all makes sense now.'

Saffie choked on her wine. 'Clare! You're such a dark horse. Come to think of it; he was all gooey-eyed when you helped him sort out that dispute over a Louboutin shoe!'

Clare shrugged. 'Guilty as charged. You two have had your share of fun with the Brooker brothers. I didn't want to be left out.'

Saffie reached for her purse. 'This calls for another round of drinks.'

*

Digby and Vivienne were having dinner at a private members' club. 'I had a meeting with Saffronella's team today. I'm very impressed with the figures. I can see her business coming on leaps and bounds over the next few years.'

Vivienne grabbed her husband's hand. 'You don't know how happy that makes me. I am so proud of Saffronella and of you for supporting her in her chosen career. I know it's not what you wanted, but your protégé is the best option by far. He's perfect.'

Digby raised his eyebrows. 'I haven't told you much about him.'

Vivienne let go of her husband's hand and picked up her knife and fork. 'I trust your judgement, my darling. I'd never interfere in the family business. I do have a question though, what if your protégé doesn't marry Saffronella? Does that mean it won't be our family business any longer? It's something that's been bothering me.'

Digby patted his wife's hand. 'There's no need to worry. We won't have a problem with that. It's about time you both met him. He's doing well with his training.'

Vivienne cringed. 'That would be lovely. When are you thinking of?'

'On Saturday. I've invited him over for dinner; we'll get caterers in. He may as well start making himself at home.'

23

MEET THE PARENTS

Digby was intrigued to see how the day would go. His wife and daughter had kept quiet about their little trip to his office in January. However, Simon, who was as loyal as a Labrador, had advised him of the strange escapade. Digby thought one of them would have come clean by now, or at least tripped up. He chuckled when he thought back to the meal at the private members' club earlier in the week – Vivienne had nearly let the cat out of the bag then. She must be having kittens today; she'd never been a good liar.

Digby walked into the dining room where his wife was arranging vases of flowers. She'd been jittery all morning. 'Digby! I thought you should sit opposite Saffronella, Simon can sit next to her, and I'll sit opposite him, next to you.'

Digby suppressed a chuckle. 'How do you know his name?'

Vivienne raised her eyes to the ceiling. 'He's been your protégé for ages now. You've mentioned him by name.' Digby knew he hadn't, but he let his wife squirm. It served her right for being so nosy.

Saffronella entered the room armed with a set of Italian placemats. 'I thought we should use these. We can always talk about the images on them if we're stuck for things to say.' Saffie glanced at her father. 'Mummy and I know nothing about Real Estate. He'll feel at home if we chat about the Rialto Bridge or the Trevi Fountain.'

Digby noticed his wife glare at their daughter. He just knew it – another slip up, and it was only half-past-ten in the morning. He pretended not to notice and took the opportunity to make himself scarce for a few hours. 'I'll leave you to it. It's a good day for golf.'

Vivienne let out a sigh of relief. 'Great idea, we can manage. Have a good game.'

*

By six o'clock, Vivienne was checking her watch. 'Your father should be home by now. He needs to shower and change before Simon arrives.'

Saffie raised her arms in the air. 'What's the

problem? I'm struggling to understand why you're making such a big fuss about this. We've met Simon already; he didn't give away our secret, and we only need to meet him officially once. We've come to terms with the business going out of the family when Daddy retires. Just chill out and have a glass of sherry. It'll only be the "meet and greet" that'll be awkward. After that, we can ask him about Italy. At least we've got the "heads up" on that.'

Vivienne's head was thumping. Not only was she keeping a secret from her husband, but she was also keeping one from her daughter. Digby would not be amused if Saffronella and Simon didn't get married; he'd put so much effort into arranging for everything to be perfect. She knew the family business was his life – without it, retirement would be a long-drawn-out affair. Vivienne wanted to cry.

'I'm back! I parred two holes. There's a competition next week, so I'm going in for it. Things are looking up! I'll have a shower and change. Simon will be here at seven – he's always prompt.'

Right on cue, the CCTV identified Simon's car at the electric gates, and Vivienne pressed a button to let him in. Digby rushed into the room and poured himself a gin and tonic. He took a large slurp before jogging to the main door to greet his guest. 'Simon! The girls are waiting for you. I've kept our secret. They don't know you told me about their little excursion to my office.' Digby slapped Simon's back. 'It's great to have you onboard!'

Vivienne and Saffie shook hands with Simon without meeting his eyes. Digby revelled in their awkwardness – it served the pair of them right. He wasn't going to dig them out of a hole; they could suffer for a while with having to make polite conversation. Digby sat back to watch the show.

After a glass or two of wine, Vivienne and Saffie were warming to the protégé. Simon was charming and well educated. They were intrigued by his recollection of childhood holidays in Italy and his evident love of the family business. Vivienne scrutinised Simon's body language for signs of chemistry with her daughter. It would be good if he put an arm around the back of Saffronella's chair – that would be a start.

During the dessert course, one of the caterers had a quiet word with Digby. He jumped up and rushed to a window. 'Oh my goodness! Something extraordinary is happening in the garden.'

Vivienne and Saffie jumped up too. Vivienne screamed. 'There's smoke everywhere – it must be a fire!'

It was Saffie's turn to scream. 'What's that wandering around over there? It looks like a ghost.'

Digby opened a sideboard drawer and pulled out his

binoculars. 'Let me see. You're right. It's a ghost!'

Vivienne felt relieved. 'It's not a fire then. It's something out of this world.'

Digby frowned at his wife. How much had she had to drink? Saffie grabbed the binoculars from her father. She took a long look, a very long look, at the ghost with a camera around its neck. It was the same ghost who had saved her when she'd set off a smoke machine facing in the wrong direction at Halloween. The ghost that day was supposed to be a lady, but thinking back, it had kept its words to a minimum and had a squeaky voice.

Saffie's heart pounded. 'There's no need to panic. I know who the ghost is. I'll go outside to speak with him.'

Saffie thumped the ghost on his shoulder. 'What are you doing? You get my hopes up on Christmas Day, then you disappear for three months, and now you're trespassing on my parents' property.'

The ghost removed its costume. 'Trust me. I'm not trespassing.'

Saffie stamped her foot, but the sight of Ben with his hair standing on end was hilarious, and she struggled not to laugh.

'Let me come and meet your parents. I want to do

it properly this time.'

'My father doesn't approve of you.'

'I can win him round.'

'You're far too big-headed for your own good.'

'I know.'

Saffie led Ben into the dining room to the sight of her parents and Simon holding glasses of champagne. Digby raised his glass in the air. 'Meet my protégé. His name's Benjamin Brooker.'

24

ALL IS REVEALED

Saffie's eyes were alight, and she couldn't take them off Ben. Vivienne let the chemistry between them warm her heart. She didn't know whether to be annoyed or delighted with Digby. He'd put her through trauma these past few months, but he'd got the best result.

Digby pulled his wife to one side. 'Do you remember when our daughter was a little girl, and we tried to show her what was best for her? She always went off in a different direction.'

Vivienne nodded. 'I do.'

'Well, this time, I've tried reverse psychology. I gave Saffronella a hard time at the start about her business, *and* I told her I disapproved of Benjamin.'

Vivienne giggled. 'You've been so clever.'

'I know.'

Vivienne frowned. 'How did you manage to link up with Benjamin? He's a videographer.'

'He's dabbled in Real Estate too for the last ten years. His late father was a competitor of mine. Benjamin wanted to make his own way in the world, but he couldn't resist the lure of Real Estate – it's in his genes. His brother, on the other hand, is best suited to photography.' Digby took a sip of champagne before continuing, 'After Benjamin's father died, he had the good sense to contact me to suggest a merger of our two companies. We'll be stronger working together than on opposing teams.'

Vivienne raised an eyebrow. 'Did you try reverse psychology on Benjamin too?'

Digby smiled. 'I certainly did. I told him Saffronella was off limits and that his priority was to make me a happy man. He's been doing his best to impress me by travelling to our offices globally. I'm pleased to say he's already identified significant business improvements.'

Vivienne wasn't surprised by her husband's tactics. 'I've always said that "absence makes the heart grow fonder". Remember when you opened the firm's South American branch soon after we met? The six weeks you spent in Argentina made me miss you terribly. The time apart sealed our relationship.'

Digby coughed as he fiddled with his cravat. That brought back memories of the Argentine Tango. Those six weeks away from Vivienne had flown by. 'Exactly!'

'Do you think Benjamin wants to marry our daughter?'

'I have no doubt. We had a conversation a couple of weeks ago. Benjamin asked me for access to Saffronella – or the company merger was off. I knew then it was time to step away from my game playing. It was a pretty good game, though. Eton served me well.'

Vivienne's heart pounded with excitement. There was still a loose end she couldn't tie up, though, and that was the young man in the dining room. 'But what about Simon? You said your protégé had black hair, green eyes, and good teeth.'

Digby chuckled. 'I needed to throw you off the scent. I didn't know when I described Simon, instead of Benjamin, that you'd bump into him so soon.'

'What?! He told you we came into the office?'

'He certainly did. He's not my Executive Assistant for nothing. He tells me everything; he's my eyes and ears in that office.'

'Are you mad at me?'

'Let's call it quits. I've been less than truthful with you over the last few months. Christmas was tough, I wanted to sample some Scotch whisky with Benjamin, and I had to pretend I didn't like him. There's an idea – we could have a wee dram now. You won't mind if he stays the night, would you?'

Vivienne gulped. 'Not at all.'

*

Simon had presents for Saffie and her mother. He held them aloft. 'I heard you had trouble getting into our office building. I've arranged for visitor passes for you both. You're welcome to pop in for a coffee any time you're in Canary Wharf.'

Digby walked over to shake Simon's hand. 'Thanks for going through with this, Simon. I don't normally keep secrets from my family – they're out in the open now. We can make an announcement next week about the company merger. I know you've got a hot date later. Please feel free to make a quick getaway.'

Saffie stared at her father. 'Company merger?'

Digby poured Scotch whisky from a decanter before handing a glass to Ben. 'Let's go and sit by the fire in the living room. We need to update Saffronella on our plans.'

*

At ten-thirty, Digby and Vivienne made a discreet exit leaving Saffie and Ben on their own. Saffie fiddled with the charms on her silver bracelet, which she'd put on after the identity of the ghost had been revealed. Her head was spinning. Ben reached into his pocket and pulled out a charm. He handed it to Saffie. She laughed. 'It's a ghost!'

Ben nodded. 'That's right. That was a turning point for us.' He reached into his pocket again and produced another charm.

'A house.'

'That's a symbol of my new career in Real Estate.' Another charm followed.

'A tiny ring.'

Ben smiled. 'I'm all out of charms now.'

Saffie's heart pounded. 'What does the ring symbolise?'

Ben reached into his pocket again. This time he produced a small box which he opened to divulge a large solitaire diamond ring. 'Hopefully, it'll symbolise that we're engaged to be married.'

Ben dropped down onto one knee. 'Will you marry me, Saffronella? If you do, I'll hire your team to plan our wedding.'

Saffie burst into tears as she nodded and held out her hand. 'We will be invoicing for our services at full cost – we don't do mates rates.'

Ben pulled Saffie to her feet. 'It's a deal. I wouldn't expect anything less from the boss.'

*

The following morning, Clare and Sophie were in shock. Saffie and Ben were getting married in June, in a local church, with a marquee in the grounds of Saffie's parents' house.

Sophie pulled at her hair. 'We've not hired a marquee before. I need to check that Dean can be the videographer.'

Clare scribbled on a notepad. 'He's not available.'

'How do you know?'

'He'll be the Best Man.'

Sophie sighed. 'You do realise this will be a nightmare? Saffie's mind won't be on anything until after her wedding. She won't be of any help on the day, and we've got four weddings in the diary to manage before the Wedding of the Year. We'll never cope.'

Clare looked up from her notes. 'Peacock food! We'll need to attract the peacocks. Saffie will screw if we don't get any in the shots.'

Sophie's phone buzzed, and she read a message from Saffie before staring at Clare. 'We need to lock the office up straight away and go wedding dress shopping with Saffie and Vivienne. I told you, didn't I? This is going to be a disaster.'

Clare took a deep breath. 'It's only for three months. Just think how happy Saffie will be when she gets back from her honeymoon. She's been like a bear with a sore head since Christmas. We've been doing more than our share of the work already.'

Sophie raised her eyes. 'What's new?!'

25

THE WEDDING OF THE YEAR

Sophie and Clare sipped champagne in Saffie's bedroom. They didn't usually drink while on duty, but today was different – they were bridesmaids too. Clare smoothed down the skirt of her violet satin dress. 'Saffie's been clever here. Our dresses will bring out the colour of her eyes.'

Sophie giggled. 'Violet looks good on you too. Heinrich will be gobsmacked when he sees you walk down the aisle.'

Clare looked out of the window. 'Where is Saffie, anyway? She went down to check on the marquee over an hour ago. It's time she got dressed.'

*

Saffie and Vivienne were seated at the top table in their dressing gowns. Vivienne held her daughter's hand. 'I've dreamt of this day for so long, but now it's here I'm a wreck. I can't believe your father will be giving you away in less than an hour. It'll break his heart.'

Saffie smiled. 'Oh, mother! Don't be so silly. You need to view it that you're gaining a son, not losing a daughter.'

Vivienne blew her nose. 'I couldn't wish for a better son than Benjamin.'

Saffie sniggered. 'You're lucky I didn't fall for Rufus.'

Vivienne's eyes widened. 'The one that ended up in prison? That was such a shame for Eloise Bloomfield. Still, it was a bonus the penthouse apartment fell through. Your father always had his eyes set on that for you.'

Saffie blushed. 'I can't believe Daddy has given it to us as a wedding present.'

Vivienne hugged her daughter. 'He had an ulterior motive. You won't be too far away from us living in the West End. Now, come along, we should get dressed. The cars will be here in twenty minutes.'

*

Ben and Dean stood outside the church greeting their

guests. The flowers adorning an arch around the church entrance were bursting with colour. Ben could smell the lilac freesias, peach roses, cream magnolias, and pink carnations. His heart was filled with pride as he turned to his brother. 'Mum and Dad would have loved her.'

Dean's eyes glistened. 'They certainly would.' Dean swallowed before continuing, 'Are you sure I can't do the filming today? I'll be at a loss.'

Ben smiled. 'It's your day off. You need to look after Sophie. That's after you've done your Best Man speech, of course.'

Dean rummaged in his pocket for his notes. 'Thank goodness I didn't leave them at home. We were in a rush earlier. Have you got the rings?'

Ben's heart sank. 'I gave them to you.'

A wedding car drew up outside the church, and Dean grabbed his brother's arm. 'That'll be Vivienne with the bridesmaids. We should go inside. Saffie and Digby won't be too far behind; it'll be unlucky if you see her before she walks down the aisle.'

Ben forced a smile at the guests as he sat down in the front pew. He whispered to Dean, 'What are we going to do about the rings?'

Dean reached into his pocket and pulled out a small

box. 'Only joking. Just wait until you hear my speech later. *That's* something you should be worried about.'

Vivienne waited outside the church to see her husband and daughter arrive before making her way down the aisle. She smiled at the sea of faces and was pleased to see Ben wink at her as she took her seat. He mouthed the words, 'I love your hat'. Vivienne tilted it slightly to the right as the lady in the mother-of-the-bride shop had recommended.

With the vicar in place, the organist began to play *Here Comes the Bride*. The congregation stood up, and Ben's knees went weak. The brothers faced the front of the church. Dean took a crafty look behind before whispering to Ben, 'She didn't stand you up. It's definitely her.' Ben wiped his clammy hands on his trousers and turned to face his bride. He gulped at the sight of Saffie in her short white skater dress. She smiled at him with her violet eyes sparkling. 'I couldn't find anything better.'

Ben's nerves lifted, and he took her into his arms. 'It's perfect – just perfect. You look amazing.'

The vicar coughed. 'Shall we commence the ceremony?'

*

The church bells rang as Ben and Saffie strolled outside into the sunshine. Dean walked out of the church with

Sophie. 'Did you bring my camera?'

Sophie searched for Heinrich, who was looking after the bridesmaids' handbags. She rushed over to him, then back to Dean. 'Here it is.'

Dean combed a hand through his unruly blonde hair. 'Great! I know I'm not on duty, but no one knows my brother and Saffie better than me. I've done a trial run of their best wedding shots already.'

Sophie raised her eyes. 'While I went to the loch on Christmas Day and ended up with frozen feet.'

Dean adjusted his lens. 'Exactly! A good decision by me.'

Sophie glanced sideways at the ardent photographer. 'It depends how you view it. There was no one at the loch to take photos of the monster.'

Dean's head spun around. 'You saw a monster?!'

Sophie looked into his eyes. 'We certainly did. It was the fairies who stole the show, though.'

'The fairies?!'

'Yep. They were having a ride on the monster's back while drinking champagne and eating Christmas pudding.'

Dean burst out laughing. 'I do love you, Sophie.

You've got the same sense of humour as me!'

'You *love* me?'

Dean blushed. 'Well, that may be the wrong word to use. You're a good mate. Yes, that's what it is — you're a good mate to have around.'

Digby stood tall and proud. What an achievement! He glanced over at Vivienne, who looked stunning in her hat. As soon as he'd handed the family business over to Benjamin, he would travel the world on holiday with his wife rather than on business trips. There was so much to look forward to in retirement.

An open-top carriage arrived outside the church, pulled by four white horses. The guests cheered and threw handfuls of confetti over the happy couple. Saffie extracted biodegradable rose petals from her cleavage. 'I feel like Cinderella.'

Ben grinned. Saffie was far better than Cinderella — she was real, and she was his. As far as Ben was concerned, he'd won the Star Prize.

26

A RECEPTION TO REMEMBER

The dancefloor was crowded, and Dean was the centre of attention as he performed a robot dance before grabbing hold of Sophie and swinging her into a tango pose. 'Did you like my speech?'

Sophie giggled. 'It was hilarious. Who would have known that Ben enjoyed playing with Barbie dolls when he was younger, while you went to rugby?'

Dean twirled her around. 'He didn't. That was just a figment of my imagination. I've got my own back on him now for being the macho brother. People will look at us differently in future.'

Sophie laughed. 'You are the worst brother anyone could have.'

'I'm hopefully not the worst boyfriend, though.'

Sophie shrugged. 'I wouldn't know.'

Dean winked. 'Would you like to find out?'

Sophie sighed. 'I guess I'll have to. It's tradition for the Best Man to run off with a bridesmaid.'

Heinrich was trying to do a waltz with Clare. 'You must have time for a holiday soon. I want to take you to Germany. We should go on a river cruise down the Rhine.'

Clare looked up at him. 'After the extra hours I've put in to get this wedding off the ground, I deserve some time off. Let me know the dates, and I'll be there.'

Ben and Saffie sat on a bench overlooking the lake. He couldn't take his eyes off her. She looked stunning with a coronet of flowers on her head. 'You should wear flowers in your hair all the time, Mrs Brooker.'

Saffie grinned at her husband. 'Mrs Saffronella Brooker. I'll have to get used to that. I'm not sure about you wearing pink fluffy slippers around our new apartment, though – they'll have to go.'

Ben chuckled. 'Don't believe everything Dean said in his speech.'

Saffie lowered her eyes. 'He said he'd never seen

you so happy since you met me.'

Ben leant forward to kiss his bride. 'Now that part is true.'

The romantic moment was interrupted by honking and screaming. Saffie and Ben turned around to witness five peacocks running towards them. Saffie looked down at the grass. 'We're sitting in the middle of Clare's peacock feeding area. They won't be happy with us!'

Ben threw an arm under Saffie's legs and picked her up. She clung to his neck as he jogged to the safety of the house. He was out of breath when they got there. Saffie giggled. 'You're not very fit, Mr Brooker. I hope you've got enough energy left to cut the cake.'

Ben's eyes twinkled as he placed Saffie's feet on the ground. He clung onto her with one hand and straightened the flowers in her hair with the other. He then bent forward to finish their kiss. It was now Saffie's turn to suffer from weak knees. Ben brushed her cheek with his fingers before gazing into her eyes. 'As far as you're concerned, Mrs Brooker, I have all the energy in the world.'

A cough came from behind. 'Excuse me, Sir. Your cars are here.'

Ben held Saffie at arm's length. 'We have unfinished business. Meet me at the Tower of London in . . .' Ben looked at his watch. 'In about twenty minutes' time. I'll jump into my car first. Give me a head start. No one will miss us.' Ben kissed Saffie before he rushed off.

Saffie spoke to her driver, who was waiting outside a silver Bentley. 'I just need to pop into the house. I won't be long.' She returned ten minutes later wearing the silver dress. 'We'd best go. I wouldn't want my husband to be waiting for me for too long. I'll be late as it is.'

Fifteen minutes later, Saffie was panicking. 'I'm sure we're going the wrong way. We should be there by now.'

The driver looked in his rear-view mirror. 'It's because of the roadworks.'

Fifteen minutes after that, Saffie stepped out of the car and walked to the area where she had waited for Ben last year. He wasn't there. She stood rooted to the spot for another ten minutes before she looked down at her dress and wanted to cry. Why had she gone back to change? The dress was unlucky after all – she hung her head. Suddenly a strong arm slid around her waist from behind, and she could smell his aftershave.

'You wore the dress.'

Saffie turned around, and Ben produced a bunch of pink roses from behind his back. She cried with relief. 'Where were you going to take me that night?'

'On a boat for a private dinner for two.'

Saffie squeezed her husband. 'That would have been lovely.'

Ben took hold of her hand and guided her towards the quayside. 'Unfortunately, our boat trip won't be so intimate this time.'

Saffie looked over at a huge party boat containing their whistling and cheering wedding guests. Ben glanced at his watch and turned to face his wife. Thankfully tonight, you've arrived at the perfect time. He held Saffie in front of him as a cascade of fireworks lit up the sky. Saffie could see Clare and Sophie jumping up and down on the boat, and she waved her flowers in the air.

Sophie's mouth fell open before she disappeared from the deck. Minutes later, she returned with Saffie's wedding bouquet before shouting: 'You're not getting away without throwing this. Just aim at me and make sure it doesn't fall into the Thames.'

Ben smiled down at his bride. 'Trust Sophie to think of everything. We should get onto the boat. Of course, you could always throw the flowers to Clare.'

Saffie grinned. She wasn't going to throw her bouquet to anyone; she knew who deserved it the most.

*

The following morning, Heinrich walked into the Lavender Tree Banqueting Rooms carrying Saffie's bouquet. He handed it to Rebecca. 'Saffronella asked me to give this to you.'

Rebecca's eyes lit up as she read the note from Saffie:

Dear Rebecca

Clare mentioned you've been dating that very handsome blonde barman at the Lavender Tree Banqueting Rooms for nearly a year now.

I know you're superstitious, so I'm sending you my wedding bouquet to help things along.

Wishing you all the happiness in the world!

Love Saffronella x

****

Printed in Great Britain
by Amazon

79205771R00099